Discard
Keepat
home

Eric

HOUGHTON MIFFLIN Science
Florida

 HOUGHTON MIFFLIN   BOSTON

Program Authors

William Badders
Director of the Cleveland Mathematics
and Science Partnership
Cleveland Municipal School District
Cleveland, Ohio

Douglas Carnine, Ph.D.
Professor of Education
University of Oregon
Eugene, Oregon

James Feliciani
Supervisor of Instructional
Media and Technology
Land O' Lakes, Florida

Bobby Jeanpierre, Ph.D.
Assistant Professor, Science Education
University of Central Florida
Orlando, Florida

Carolyn Sumners, Ph.D.
Director of Astronomy and Physical Sciences
Houston Museum of Natural Science
Houston, Texas

Catherine Valentino
Author-in-Residence
Houghton Mifflin
West Kingston, Rhode Island

Content Consultants

Dr. Robert Arnold
Professor of Biology
Colgate University
Hamilton, New York

Dr. Carl D. Barrentine
Associate Professor of Humanities
and Biology
University of North Dakota
Grand Forks, North Dakota

Dr. Steven L. Bernasek
Department of Chemistry
Princeton University
Princeton, New Jersey

Dennis W. Cheek
Senior Manager
Science Applications International
Corporation
Exton, Pennsylvania

Dr. Jung Choi
School of Biology
Georgia Tech
Atlanta, Georgia

Prof. John Conway
Department of Physics
University of California
Davis, California

Printed in the U.S.A.

ISBN-13: 978-0-618-62447-8
ISBN-10: 0-618-62447-3

4 5 6 7 8 9-DW-14 13 12 11 10 09 08 07

Content Consultants

Dr. Robert Dailey
Division of Animal and Veterinary Sciences
West Virginia University
Morgantown, West Virginia

Dr. Thomas Davies
IODP/USIO Science Services
Texas A & M University
College Station, Texas

Dr. Ron Dubreuil
Department of Biological Sciences
University of Illinois at Chicago
Chicago, Illinois

Dr. Orin G. Gelderloos
Professor of Biology
University of Michigan - Dearborn
Dearborn, Michigan

Dr. Michael R. Geller
Associate Professor, Department of Physics
University of Georgia
Athens, Georgia

Dr. Erika Gibb
Department of Physics
Notre Dame University
South Bend, Indiana

Dr. Fern Gotfried
Pediatrician
Hanover Township, New Jersey

Dr. Michael Haaf
Chemistry Department
Ithaca College
Ithaca, New York

Professor Melissa A. Hines
Department of Chemistry
Cornell University
Ithaca, New York

Dr. Jonathan M. Lincoln
Assistant Provost & Dean of Undergraduate Education
Bloomsburg University
Bloomsburg, Pennsylvania

Donald Lisowy
Wildlife Conservation Society
Bronx Zoo
Bronx, New York

Dr. Marc L. Mansfield
Department of Chemistry and Chemical Biology
Stevens Institute of Technology
Hoboken, New Jersey

Dr. Scott Nuismer
Department of Biological Sciences
University of Idaho
Moscow, Idaho

Dr. Suzanne O'Connell
Department of Earth and Environmental Sciences
Wesleyan University
Middletown, Connecticut

Dr. Kenneth Parsons
Assistant Professor of Meteorology
Embry-Riddle Aeronautical University
Prescott, Arizona

Betty Preece
Engineer and Physicist
Indialantic, Florida

Dr. Chantal Reid
Department of Biology
Duke University
Durham, North Carolina

Dr. Todd V. Royer
Department of Biological Sciences
Kent State University
Kent, Ohio

Dr. Kate Scholberg
Physics Department
Duke University
Durham, North Carolina

Dr. Jeffery Scott
Department of Earth, Atmospheric, and Planetary Sciences
Massachusetts Institute of Technology
Cambridge, Massachusetts

Dr. Ron Stoner
Professor Emeritus, Physics and Astronomy Department
Bowling Green State University
Bowling Green, Ohio

Dr. Dominic Valentino, Ph.D.
Professor, Department of Psychology
University of Rhode Island
Kingston, Rhode Island

Dr. Sidney White
Professor Emeritus of Geology
Ohio State University
Columbus, Ohio

Dr. Scott Wissink
Professor, Department of Physics
Indiana University
Bloomington, Indiana

Dr. David Wright
Department of Chemistry
Vanderbilt University
Nashville, Tennessee

Contents

UNIT A Plants, Animals, and People

Reading in Science A2

Chapter 1 **Plants** A4

Lesson 1 . . . . A6

Lesson 2 . . . . A12

Focus On: Technology A18

Lesson 3 . . . . A20

Review and SAT 10 Practice A26

Chapter 2 **Animals** A28

Lesson 1 . . . . A30

Focus On: Literature A36

Lesson 2 . . . . A38

Lesson 3 . . . . A44

Review and SAT 10 Practice A50

Chapter 3 **People** A52

Lesson 1 . . . . A54

Focus On: Health and Safety A60

Lesson 2 . . . . A62

Review and SAT 10 Practice A70

Unit A Wrap-Up A72

UNIT B · Living Things and Where They Live

Reading in Science B2

Chapter 4 **Living Things** B4

Lesson 1 . . . . .B6

Focus On: Readers' Theater B12

Lesson 2 . . . . .B14

Review and SAT 10 Practice B22

Chapter 5 **Where Plants and Animals Live** B24

Lesson 1 . . . . .B26

Lesson 2 . . . . .B32

Focus On: Biography B38

Lesson 3 . . . . .B40

Review and SAT 10 Practice B46

Unit B Wrap-Up B48

Contents

UNIT C Earth, Our Home

Reading in Science C2

Chapter 6 **Looking at Our Earth** C4

Lesson 1 .C6

Lesson 2 .C12

Focus On: Readers' Theater C18

Lesson 3 .C22

Review and SAT 10 Practice C28

Chapter 7 **Caring for Our Earth** C30

Lesson 1 .C32

Lesson 2 .C38

Focus On: Health and Safety C44

Lesson 3 .C46

Review and SAT 10 Practice C54

Unit C Wrap-Up C56

Weather and the Sky

Reading in Science D2

Chapter 8 **Weather and Seasons** D4

Lesson 1 . . . . D6

Lesson 2 . . . . D12

Focus On: Literature D18

Lesson 3 . . . . D20

Lesson 4 . . . . D26

Lesson 5 . . . . D32

Review and SAT 10 Practice D40

Chapter 9 **Changes in the Sky** D42

Lesson 1 . . . . D44

Lesson 2 . . . . D50

Lesson 3 . . . . D56

Focus On: Biography D62

Lesson 4 . . . . D64

Review and SAT 10 Practice D70

Unit D Wrap-Up D72

Contents

UNIT E Describing Matter

Reading in Science E2

Chapter 10 Observing Objects E4

Lesson 1 . . . . .E6

Lesson 2 . . . . .E12

Lesson 3 . . . . .E18

Focus On: Technology E24

Lesson 4 . . . . .E26

Review and SAT 10 Practice E32

Chapter 11 Changes in Matter E34

Lesson 1 . . . . .E36

Lesson 2 . . . . .E42

Focus On: Literature E47

Lesson 3 . . . . .E48

Review and SAT 10 Practice E54

Unit E Wrap-Up E56

UNIT F Energy Sources and Motion

Reading in Science F2

Chapter 12 **Heat, Light, and Sound** F4

Lesson 1 . . . . .F6

Lesson 2 . . . . .F12

Lesson 3 . . . . .F18

Focus On: Technology F23

Lesson 4 . . . . .F24

Review and SAT 10 Practice F30

Chapter 13 **Moving Faster and Slower** F32

Lesson 1 . . . . .F34

Lesson 2 . . . . .F40

Focus On: Readers' Theater F46

Lesson 3 . . . . .F48

Review and SAT 10 Practice F54

Unit F Wrap-Up F56

Features

UNIT A

Investigate Activities

Observe a Plant A7
Compare Leaves A13
Use Plant Models A21
Hidden Animals A31
Classify Animals A39
A Cat's Life Cycle A45
Model Your Body A55
A Person's Life A63

Reading in Science

What's Alive? by Kathleen Weidner
   Zoehfeld A2

Focus On

Technology: Plant Power! A18
Literature: "In a Winter Meadow";
   Animal Disguises A36
Health and Safety:
   Florida Activity Trails A60

UNIT B

Investigate Activities

Classify Objects B7
Observe Plants B15
Observe a Tree B27
Compare Animals B33
Wet or Dry B41

Reading in Science

Over in the Meadow
   by Ezra Jack Keats B2

Focus On

Readers' Theater:
   Living or Nonliving? B12
Biography: Marjory Stoneman
   Douglas B38

UNIT C

Investigate Activities

Land and Water C7
Compare Rocks C13
Observe Soil C23
Collect Pollution C33
A Waterwheel C39
Sort Your Trash C47

Reading in Science

Dirt by Steve Tomecek C2

Focus On

Readers' Theater: Rock Stars . .C18
Health and Safety:
   Safety at the Beach C44

UNIT D

Investigate Activities
Record Weather D7
Measure Weather D13
Water Changes D21
Grow Plants D27
What to Wear D33
Observe the Sky D45
Day and Night D51

Moon Changes D57
Sun Changes D65

Reading in Science
What Will the Weather Be?
  by Lynda DeWitt D2

Focus On
Literature: *Rain;* "City Rain" . . . D18
Biography: Neil Armstrong D62

UNIT E

Investigate Activities
Classify Objects E7
Use Tools E13
Use Magnets E19
Float or Sink E27
Compare Matter E37
Predict Changes E43
Make a Mixture E49

Reading in Science
What Is the World Made Of?
  by Kathleen Weidner
  Zoehfeld E2

Focus On
Technology: Mighty Magnets . . E24
Literature: *Big Freeze* E47

UNIT F

Investigate Activities
Measure Heat F7
Shine Light F13
Make Sounds F19
Different Sounds F25
How Things Move F35
Compare Distance F41
Change Motion F49

Reading in Science
Energy: Heat, Light, and Fuel
  by Darlene Stille F2

Focus On
Technology: Thump, Thump! . . . F23
Readers' Theater:
  A Wild Ride F46

How Your Book Is Organized

The Nature of Science

In the front of your book you will learn about how people explore science.

Units

The major sections of your book are units.

Unit Title tells you what the unit is about.

Find more information related to this unit from the creators of Cricket magazine, on the EduPlace web site.

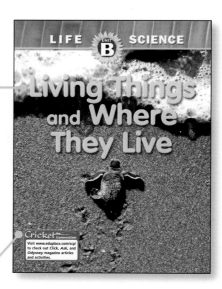

Reading in Science gives you something to think and talk about.

Chapters are parts of a unit. This tells you what the chapters are about.

You can read these on your own.

Discover! is a question to get you started. You can answer the question when you finish the unit.

Chapter Vocabulary shows the vocabulary you will learn and gets you started.

Every lesson in your book has two parts.

Part 1: Investigate Activity

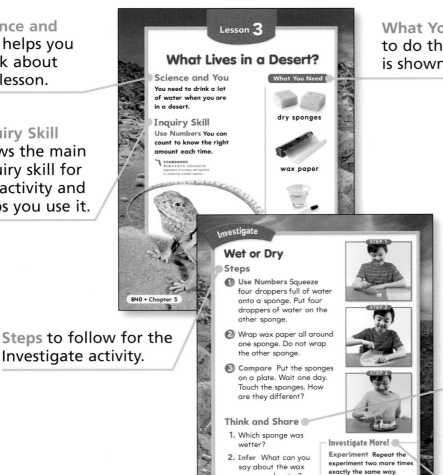

Science and You helps you think about the lesson.

Inquiry Skill shows the main inquiry skill for the activity and helps you use it.

Steps to follow for the Investigate activity.

What You Need to do the activity is shown here.

Think and Share lets you check what you have learned.

Investigate More lets you do more on your own.

Part 2: Learn by Reading

Vocabulary lists the new science words you will learn. In the text dark words with yellow around them are new words.

Main Idea is underlined to show you what is important.

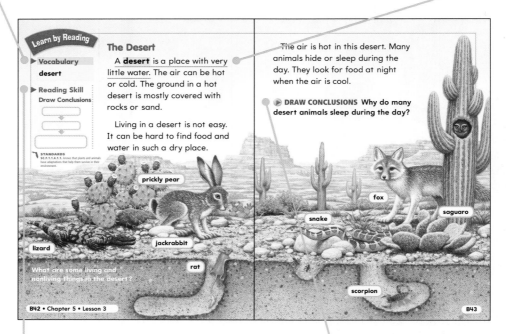

Learn by Reading

▶ **Vocabulary**
desert

▶ **Reading Skill**
Draw Conclusions

STANDARDS
SC.F.1.1.4.1.1. know that plants and animals have adaptations that help them survive in this environment.

The Desert

A **desert** is a place with very little water. The air can be hot or cold. The ground in a hot desert is mostly covered with rocks or sand.

Living in a desert is not easy. It can be hard to find food and water in such a dry place.

What are some living and nonliving things in the desert?

prickly pear

lizard

jackrabbit

rat

The air is hot in this desert. Many animals hide or sleep during the day. They look for food at night when the air is cool.

▶ **DRAW CONCLUSIONS** Why do many desert animals sleep during the day?

fox

snake

saguaro

scorpion

B42 • Chapter 5 • Lesson 3

B43

Reading Skill helps you understand the text.

Reading Skill Check has you think about what you just read.

Lesson Wrap-Up

After you read, check what you have learned.

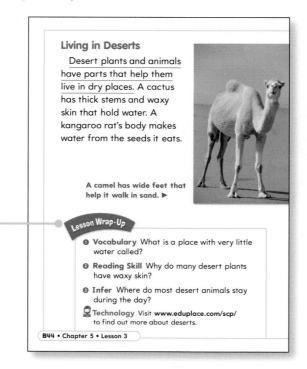

Living in Deserts

Desert plants and animals have parts that help them live in dry places. A cactus has thick stems and waxy skin that hold water. A kangaroo rat's body makes water from the seeds it eats.

A camel has wide feet that help it walk in sand. ▶

Lesson Wrap-Up

❶ **Vocabulary** What is a place with very little water called?

❷ **Reading Skill** Why do many desert plants have waxy skin?

❸ **Infer** Where do most desert animals stay during the day?

🖳 **Technology** Visit www.eduplace.com/scp/ to find out more about deserts.

B44 • Chapter 5 • Lesson 3

Focus On

Focus On lets you learn more about an important topic. Look for Biography, Technology, Literature, Readers' Theater—and more.

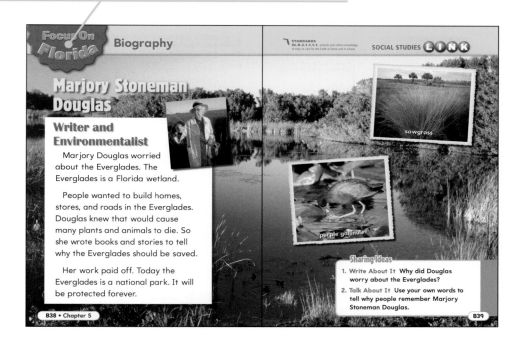

Links

Connects science to other subject areas.

You can do these at school or at home.

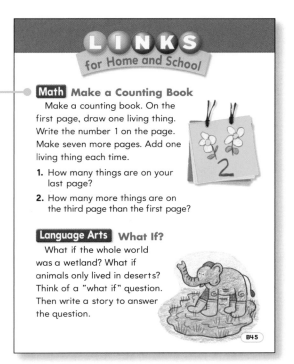

Review and Test Prep

These reviews help you to know you are on track with your learning. Here you will practice and apply your new skills.

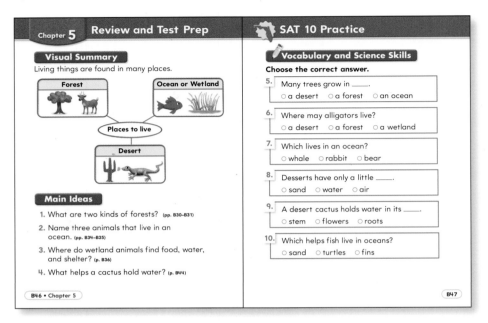

Chapter 5 | Review and Test Prep

SAT 10 Practice

Visual Summary

Living things are found in many places.

Forest

Ocean or Wetland

Places to live

Desert

Main Ideas

1. What are two kinds of forests? (pp. B30–B31)
2. Name three animals that live in an ocean. (pp. B34–B35)
3. Where do wetland animals find food, water, and shelter? (p. B36)
4. What helps a cactus hold water? (p. B44)

B46 • Chapter 5

Vocabulary and Science Skills

Choose the correct answer.

5. Many trees grow in _____.
   ○ a desert ○ a forest ○ an ocean
6. Where may alligators live?
   ○ a desert ○ a forest ○ a wetland
7. Which lives in an ocean?
   ○ whale ○ rabbit ○ bear
8. Desserts have only a little _____.
   ○ sand ○ water ○ air
9. A desert cactus holds water in its _____.
   ○ stem ○ flowers ○ roots
10. Which helps fish live in oceans?
    ○ sand ○ turtles ○ fins

B47

Unit Wrap-Up

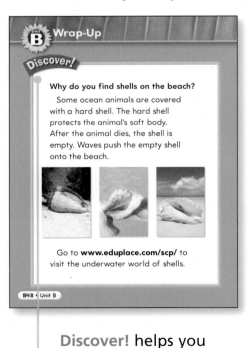

B | Wrap-Up

Discover!

Why do you find shells on the beach?

Some ocean animals are covered with a hard shell. The hard shell protects the animal's soft body. After the animal dies, the shell is empty. Waves push the empty shell onto the beach.

Go to **www.eduplace.com/scp/** to visit the underwater world of shells.

B48 • Unit B

Discover! helps you answer the question that started the unit.

References

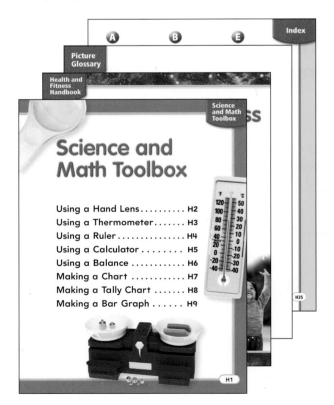

A | B | E | Index

Picture Glossary

Health and Fitness Handbook

Science and Math Toolbox

Science and Math Toolbox

Using a Hand Lens H2
Using a Thermometer H3
Using a Ruler H4
Using a Calculator H5
Using a Balance H6
Making a Chart H7
Making a Tally Chart H8
Making a Bar Graph H9

H1

The back of your book includes sections you will refer to again and again.

Florida

The Nature of Science

Science is an adventure.
People all over the world do
science. You can do science, too.
You probably already do.

Sunshine State Standards

SC.H.1.1.1.1.1. knows that scientific investigations generally work the same way in different places.

SC.H.1.1.2.1.1. understands the importance of accuracy and repetition in conducting scientific inquiries.

SC.H.1.1.3.1.1. works with others to complete an experiment or to solve a problem.

SC.H.1.1.3.1.2. listens, records, and compares the ideas and observations of others.

SC.H.3.1.1.1.1. knows that scientists and technologists use a variety of tools (e.g., thermometers, magnifiers, rulers, and scales) to obtain information in more detail and to make work easier.

The Nature of Science

You Can Do What Scientists Do . . S2

You Can Think Like a Scientist . . . S4

You Can Be an Inventor S10

You Can Make Decisions S14

Science Safety S16

Do What Scientists Do

Donna House planned this wetland and woods. Ms. House is a scientist. She studies plants and how native people use them. She protects plants that are in danger of dying out.

Donna House chose the wild plants around the National Museum of the American Indian in Washington, D.C.

Scientists Investigate

Scientists ask questions. They answer them by observing and testing. Donna House gathers facts about plants. She reads about plants. She uses tools to measure plants. She talks to other scientists. She talks to elders in different tribes.

Meet Donna House. She says you can learn a lot by taking walks outdoors with your elders.

Think Like a Scientist

Everyone can do science. To think like a scientist you have to:

- ▶ ask a lot of questions.

- ▶ work with others and listen to their ideas.

- ▶ try things over and over again.

- ▶ tell what really happens, not what you wanted to happen.

Do goldfish have eyelids? It looks like goldfish never close their eyes.

I read that goldfish do not have eyelids.

If the sunlight is too bright for their eyes, they swim to a shady spot.

Use Critical Thinking

Scientists use observations and other facts to answer their questions. A fact can be checked to make sure it is true. An opinion is what you think about the facts.

When you think, "That can't be true," you are thinking critically. Critical thinkers question what they hear.

Science Inquiry

You can use **science inquiry** to learn about the world around you. Say you are playing with magnets.

Observe It seems like when I hold the magnets one way, they push apart. When I turn one magnet, they stick.

Ask a Question I wonder, are some parts of round magnets stronger than other parts?

Form an Idea I think some parts of round magnets are stronger than others.

Experiment I will need a round magnet and some paper clips. I will count how many paper clips the round magnet picks up. I will test different places on the magnet.

Conclusion I found that a round magnet picks up more paper clips on one side. So, my idea is supported. Round magnets do have parts that are stronger.

Communicate what you learn. You can use words or pictures. Tell others to try it themselves. You can expect them to get the same results.

Inquiry Process

Here is how some scientists answer questions and make new discoveries.

```
        ┌──────────────────┐
        │     Observe      │◄──────────┐
        └────────┬─────────┘           │
                 ▼                      │
        ┌──────────────────┐           │
        │  Ask a Question  │           │
        └────────┬─────────┘           │
                 ▼                      │
        ┌──────────────────┐           │
        │   Form an Idea   │           │
        └────────┬─────────┘           │
                 ▼                      │
        ┌──────────────────┐           │
        │ Do an Experiment │           │
        └────────┬─────────┘           │
                 ▼                      │
        ┌──────────────────┐           │
        │ Draw a Conclusion│           │
        └───┬──────────┬───┘           │
            ▼          ▼               │
   ┌──────────┐   ┌──────────────┐     │
   │ Idea Is  │   │ Idea Is Not  │─────┘
   │Supported │   │  Supported   │
   └──────────┘   └──────────────┘
```

Try it Yourself!

Experiment With a Diving Squid

Squeeze the bottle. The squid sinks.
Stop squeezing. The squid floats.

1. What questions do you have about the squid?

2. How would you find the answers?

3. Make a plan to test your idea. Tell what you think you will find out.

You Can...

Be an Inventor

Neil Dermody had trouble finding his seat belt when he was eight years old. His mom asked him to invent a way to solve the problem.

First, Neil thought of putting light bulbs on the seat belt. He decided that the bulbs might break. Then he thought of things that glow in the dark.

Neil painted the buckle with paint that glowed in the dark. He sewed glow-in-the-dark fabric to the strap. It worked just fine.

Neil Dermody wins first prize for his invention.

"My mom always said, 'What problem are you having? How can you fix it?'"

What Is Technology?

The tools people make and use are **technology.** Paint that glows in the dark is technology. So is a hybrid car.

Scientists use technology. They use telescopes to study things that are far from Earth. They also use tools to measure things.

Technology can make life easier. Sometimes it causes problems too. Cars make it easy for people to travel. But a car's gas and oil can pollute the air.

A Better Idea

"I wish I had a better way to _____."
How would you fill in the blank?
Everyone can invent new things
and ideas. Even you!

An electric toothbrush
is fun to use. It also
cleans teeth better.

How to Be an Inventor

① **Find a problem.** It may be at school, at home, or in your neighborhood.

② **Think of a way to solve the problem.** List some ways to solve the problem. Decide which one will work best.

③ **Make a sample and try it out.** Your idea may need many materials or none at all. Try it out many times.

④ **Make your invention better.** Use what you learned to make changes.

⑤ **Share your invention.** Tell how your invention makes an activity easier or more fun. If it did not work well, tell why.

Make Decisions

Throwing Paper Away

How much paper does your class throw away? Most paper and other trash is buried in the ground. It takes up a lot of space.

Paper is made from mashed wood. Many trees are cut down to make paper. A lot of water is used. A lot of energy is used too.

Scrap Paper To Reuse

Deciding What to Do

How could your class throw away less paper?

Here's how to make your decision. You can use the same steps to help solve problems in your home or neighborhood.

Learn → Learn about the problem. Find the facts. You could talk to an expert or read a book.

List → List actions you could take. Add actions other people could take.

Decide → Decide which action is best for you, your school, or your neighborhood.

Share → Tell others what you decide.

Science Safety

Know the safety rules of your classroom and follow them. Follow the safety tips in your science book.

- ▶ **Wear safety goggles when your teacher tells you.**

- ▶ **Keep your work area clean. Tell your teacher about spills right away.**

- ▶ **Learn how to care for the plants and animals in your classroom.**

- ▶ **Wash your hands when you are done.**

LIFE  SCIENCE

UNIT A

Plants, Animals, and People

Florida Bird Life

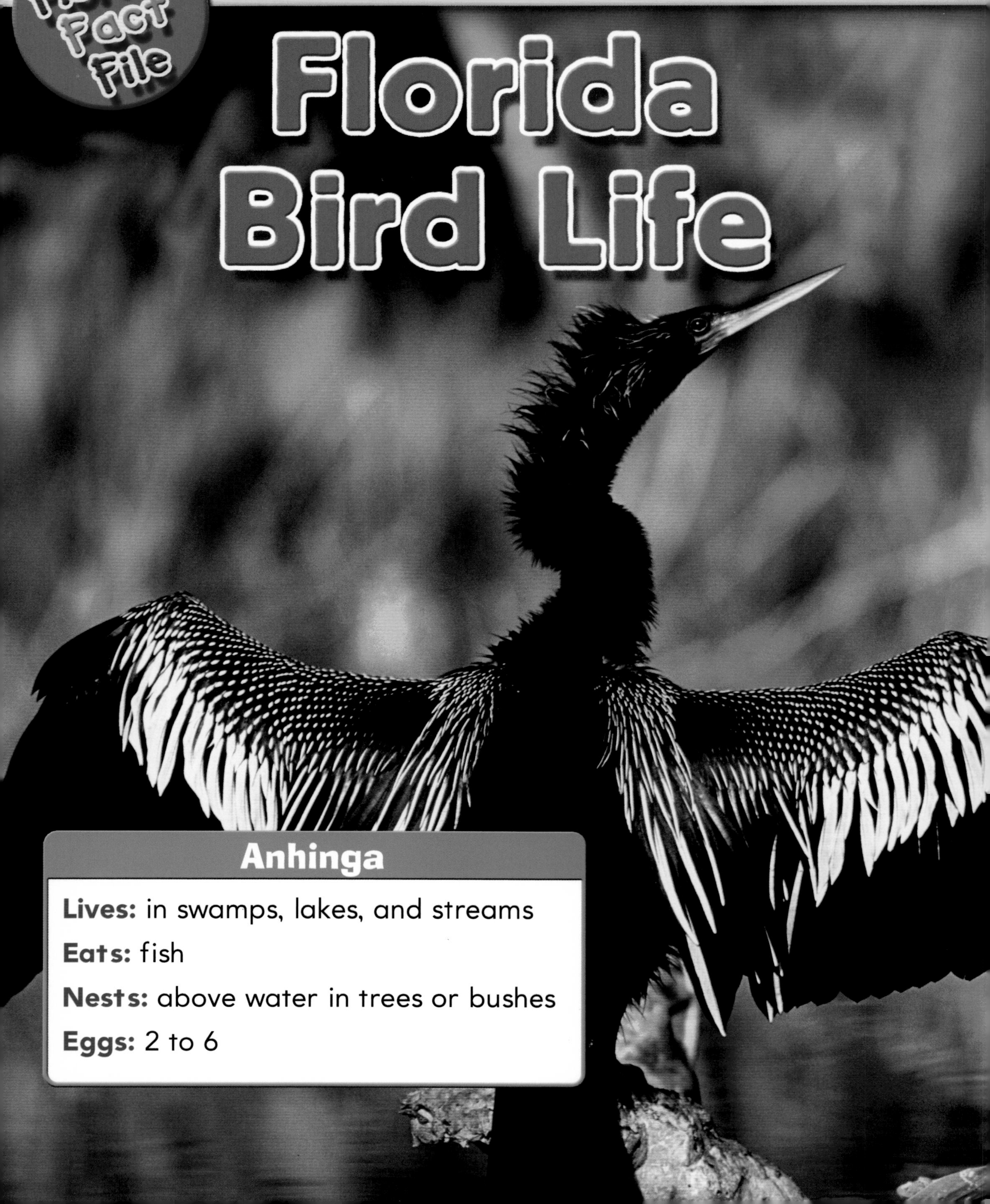

Anhinga

Lives: in swamps, lakes, and streams

Eats: fish

Nests: above water in trees or bushes

Eggs: 2 to 6

Mockingbird

Lives: near the ocean and gulf

Eats: bugs, fruit, seeds

Nests: in tree branches

Eggs: 4 to 6

Roseate Spoonbill

Lives: along the coast and in the Keys

Eats: fish

Nests: in branches above the water

Eggs: 2 to 3

Florida Scrub Jay

Lives: in central Florida

Eats: acorns and insects

Nests: in oak scrub

Eggs: 3 to 4

Sunshine State Standards

SC.A.2.1.1.1.1. knows that objects are composed of parts that are too small to be seen without magnification (for example, rocks, cookies, string, paper).

SC.B.1.1.4.1.1. knows ways that human activities require and release energy.

SC.B.1.1.5.1.1. understands that people need food for energy.

SC.B.1.1.5.1.2. knows nutritional value of various foods (for example, fruit, cereals, dairy, meat).

SC.F.1.1.3.1.1. knows ways organisms change as they grow and mature (for example, as people grow up their size changes).

SC.F.1.1.3.1.2. knows that living things grow and change in different ways and in different lengths of time (for example, butterfly, frog, daisy, pine tree).

SC.F.1.1.4.1.1. knows that plants and animals have adaptations that help them survive in their environment (camouflage, teeth, spines).

SC.F.1.1.5.1.1. understands different ways in which living things can be grouped (for example, plant/animals, edible plants/non-edible plants).

SC.F.2.1.1.1.1. knows that plants and animals are similar but not identical to their parents.

SC.F.2.1.2.1.3. knows some ways in which animals and plants are adapted to living in different environments.

SC.G.1.1.2.1.1. knows that plants produce oxygen and food for animals.

SC.G.1.1.2.1.2. understands that animals can be grouped according to what they eat.

SC.H.1.1.3.1.1. works with others to complete an experiment or to solve a problem.

SC.H.1.1.3.1.2. listens, records, and compares the ideas and observations of others.

SC.H.1.1.4.1.1. uses simple graphs, pictures, written statements, and numbers to observe, describe, record, and compare data.

SC.H.2.1.1.1.1. uses information gathered to identify patterns in nature to make predictions (for example, shapes of leaves, petals on flowers, rings on seashells).

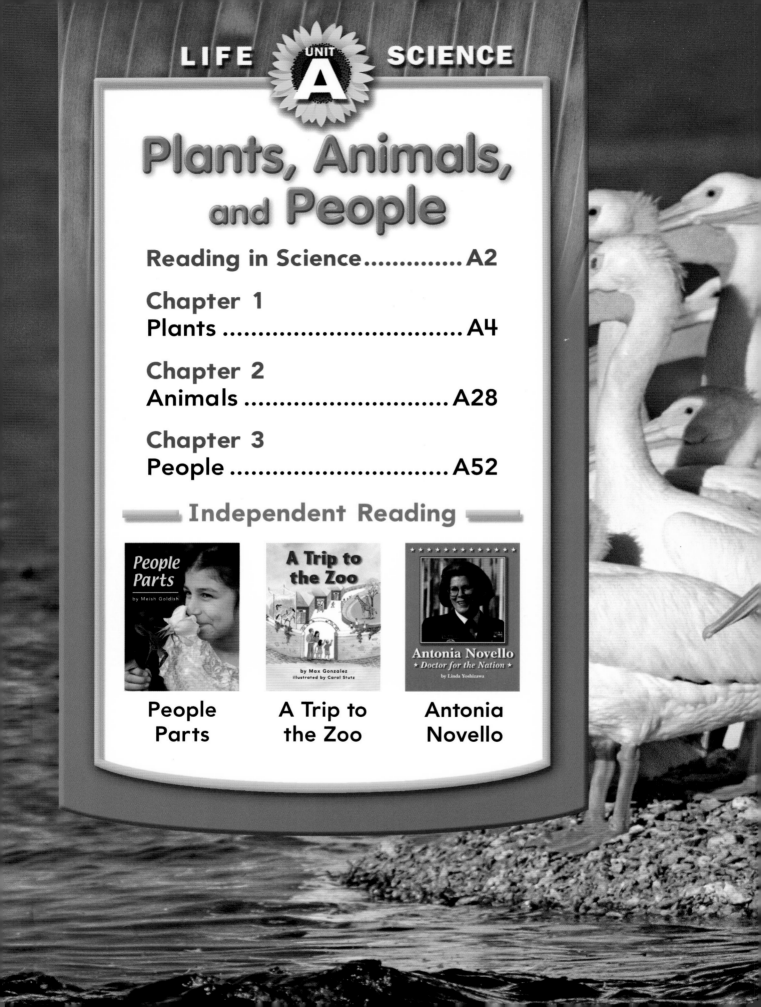

Plants, Animals, and People

Reading in Science **A2**

Chapter 1
Plants **A4**

Chapter 2
Animals **A28**

Chapter 3
People **A52**

Independent Reading

People Parts
by Meish Goldish

A Trip to the Zoo
by Max Gonzalez
illustrated by Carol Stutz

Antonia Novello
★ Doctor for the Nation ★
by Linda Yoshizawa

People
Parts

A Trip to
the Zoo

Antonia
Novello

Discover!

What bird flaps its wings
the fastest?

Think about this question as you
read. You will have the answer
by the end of the unit.

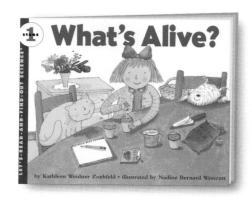

What's Alive?

by Kathleen Weidner Zoehfeld
illustrated by
Nadine Bernard Westcott

A flower can have petals of pink or yellow or red. You have no petals, and you won't grow as tall as a tree. But, like a flower and a tree, you are growing.

7

Chapter 1

Plants

roots
stem
leaves
flower
seed
spines
life cycle
cone
seedling

roots

Roots are the parts of a plant that take in water from the ground.

seed

A seed has a new plant inside it.

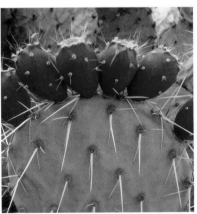

spines

A cactus has sharp points called spines.

cone

Pine seeds grow in a cone.

What Are the Parts of Plants?

Science and You

You can take better care of a plant when you know what it needs.

Inquiry Skill

Observe Use your senses to learn about things around you.

 STANDARDS
SC.H.1.1.5.1.1. uses a variety of tools (for example, thermometers, magnifiers, rulers, scales, computers) to identify characteristics of objects.

paper towels and goggles

hand lens

plant

paper and crayons

Observe a Plant

Steps

1. **Safety:** Wear goggles! Take the plant out of the pot. Carefully shake the dirt off the roots.

2. **Observe** Use a hand lens. Look at parts of the plant.

3. **Record Data** Draw a picture to show each plant part that you observe.

4. Put the plant back in the pot. **Safety:** Wash your hands!

STEP 1

STEP 2

STEP 3

Think and Share

1. What parts did you see when the plant was in the pot?

2. What part of the plant was in the soil?

Investigate More!

Ask Questions Finish the question. What would happen to the plant if it were missing its _____? Make a plan to find an answer.

Vocabulary

roots

stem

leaves

flower

seed

Reading Skill

Draw
Conclusions

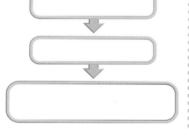

STANDARDS
SC.F.1.1.5.1.1. understands different
ways in which living things can be grouped
(for example, plant/animals, edible plants/
non-edible plants).
SC.G.1.1.2.1.1. knows that plants
produce oxygen and food for animals.

Plant Parts

Plants have parts. Most plants have roots, stems, and leaves. Some plants have flowers. Each part helps the plant in a different way.

Daisy

flower

leaf

stem

roots

Roots and Stems

Roots and stems help plants get what they need to grow. **Roots** take in water from the ground. They hold the plant in the ground.

A **stem** connects the roots to other plant parts. Stems carry water from the roots to the leaves and other plant parts. Stems also help hold a plant up.

▶ **DRAW CONCLUSIONS** How does a stem help a plant?

roots

stem

Leaves

Most plants have leaves. The **leaves** make food for the plant. Leaves give off oxygen that people and animals breathe. Some leaves are food for people and animals.

How are the leaves different?

Flowers and Seeds

Many plants have flowers. A **flower** is a part of a plant that makes seeds. A **seed** has a new plant inside it. When a seed is planted, a new plant can grow.

▶ **DRAW CONCLUSIONS** Why are seeds important?

These seeds grow in the flower.

Lesson Wrap-Up

❶ **Vocabulary** What are **roots**?

❷ **Reading Skill** Why are a plant's roots under the ground?

❸ **Observe** Which plant parts can you observe above the ground?

Technology Visit **www.eduplace.com/scp/** to find out more about plant parts.

How Can Plants Be Sorted?

Science and You

Flowers, fruits, and leaves help you know what kind of plant you have.

Inquiry Skill

Compare Look for ways that objects are alike and different.

STANDARDS
SC.H.1.1.4.1.1. uses simple graphs, pictures, written statements, and numbers to observe, describe, record, and compare data.

What You Need

leaves

paper

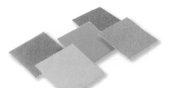

paper squares

glue and crayon

Compare Leaves

Steps

1. **Compare** Look at leaves. See how they are alike and different.

2. **Record Data** Choose three leaves that are alike in one way. Make crayon rubbings of these leaves.

3. **Classify** Glue the rubbings on a sheet of paper. Write how the leaves are alike.

4. Repeat steps 2 and 3 with different leaves.

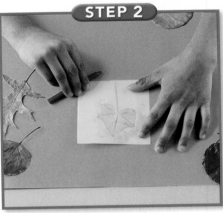

STEP 1

STEP 2

STEP 3

Think and Share

1. How are the leaves in each group alike?

2. How can you use plant parts to sort plants?

Investigate More!

Work Together Use your rubbings to make a class display. Add real leaves and pictures of leaves. Group the leaves that are alike.

STANDARDS

SC.F.1.1.5.1.1. understands different ways in which living things can be grouped (for example, plant/animals, edible plants/non-edible plants).

SC.G.1.1.2.1.1. knows that plants produce oxygen and food for animals.

Sorting Plants

You can classify plants by looking at their parts. Some plants have flowers. Some plants have flat leaves. The stem of a tree is covered with bark. A cactus has sharp points called **spines**. You can also sort plants by looking at their roots and seeds.

▶ **CLASSIFY** What are three ways to sort plants?

How could you sort these plants?

A15

Eating Plants

Some plants are food for people. Farmers grow plants. Sometimes people grow plants for food in their own gardens. You can buy food plants in a grocery store, too. These plants are safe to eat. Not all plants are safe to eat.

Plants are food for animals, too. Some animals, such as deer and rabbits, eat leaves. Squirrels and some birds eat seeds.

▶ **DRAW CONCLUSIONS** How do plants help animals?

Some birds eat fruits.

Lesson Wrap-Up

❶ **Vocabulary** What kind of plant has **spines**?

❷ **Reading Skill** What are three plant parts that animals eat?

❸ **Compare** How are plants different?

Technology Visit **www.eduplace.com/scp/** to find out more about sorting plants.

Plant Power!

People use all parts of plants—seeds, roots, stems, leaves, and flowers.

Stems Wood from the stems of trees is used to make houses— even tree houses!

STANDARDS
SC.F.1.1.5.1.1. understands different ways in which living things can be grouped (for example, plant/animals, edible plants/non-edible plants).

SOCIAL STUDIES **LINK**

Plant Parts	Things made from plant parts
Seeds The corn for your cornflakes comes from corn seeds.	cereal
Roots The roots of some beets are used to make sugar.	sugar
Leaves You use mint leaves if your toothpaste tastes like mint.	toothpaste
Flowers Many flowers are used to add pleasant smells to perfumes.	perfume

Sharing Ideas

1. **Write About It** Write a story about things in your home that are made from plant stems.

2. **Talk About It** Talk about things in your classroom that are made from plants.

How Do Plants Change as They Grow?

Science and You

You have grown from a baby to a child. Plants grow and change, too.

Inquiry Skill

Use Models Use pictures to learn about real objects.

STANDARDS
SC.H.1.1.4.1.1. uses simple graphs, pictures, written statements, and numbers to observe, describe, record, and compare data.

plant pictures

Use Plant Models

Steps

1. **Observe** Look closely at plant pictures. Think about how the plant grows.

2. **Use Models** Order the pictures to show how the plant starts, grows, and dies.

3. Make a list to show five steps in this plant's life.

Think and Share

1. What is the first step of this plant's life?

2. Describe how the plant changes through its life.

Investigate More!

Experiment Do all plants grow at the same speed? Plant two kinds of seeds at the same time. See which one grows the fastest.

Vocabulary FCAT

life cycle

cone

seedling

Reading Skill

Sequence

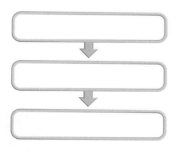

STANDARDS
SC.F.1.1.3.1.1. knows ways organisms change as they grow and mature (for example, as people grow up their size changes).
SC.F.1.1.3.1.2. knows that living things grow and change in different ways and in different lengths of time (for example, butterfly, frog, daisy, pine tree).

Pine Tree

Dandelion

Plant Life Cycles

Every living thing has a life cycle. A **life cycle** is the order of changes that happen in the lifetime of a plant or animal. The life cycle of a tree takes years. The life cycle of a dandelion only takes months. When the plants grow up, they will look like their parents.

Pine seeds grow in a **cone**.

A seed grows into a **seedling**, or a young plant.

seeds

seedling

▶ SEQUENCE How do plants change as they grow?

The seedling grows into a tree.

The tree and cones grow.

The life cycle begins again with new seeds.

growing plant

flowers grow

new seeds

◄ **6 months old**

Plant Lives

Plants live for different lengths of time. Some live only for a few months. Some plants live for about two years. Other plants live for many years.

3,000 years old ▶

Lesson Wrap-Up

❶ **Vocabulary** What is a **cone**?

❷ **Reading Skill** What comes after the seed in a plant's life cycle?

❸ **Use Models** How can a model help you learn about a plant's life cycle?

📷 **Technology** Visit **www.eduplace.com/scp/** to find out more about plant life cycles.

LINKS for Home and School

Math — Find a Pattern

Look at the pattern of the leaves.

1. What is the pattern?

2. What color is likely to come next?

Music — Sing a Plant Song

Sing these words to the tune of "The Farmer in the Dell." Then make up more verses about a plant life cycle.

The farmer plants a seed,
The farmer plants a seed,
Hi-ho, the garden-o,
The farmer plants a seed.

Visual Summary

Plants are living things. They can be grouped by plant parts.

Plant Parts

Plants have different parts.

| roots | stem | leaves | flowers |

Main Ideas

1. How do roots and stems help a plant? (p. A9)

2. How do plant leaves help people and animals? (p. A10)

3. What is one way to group plants? (p. A14)

4. How does a plant change during its life cycle? (p. A22–A23)

Vocabulary and Science Skills

Choose the correct answer.

5. Which plant part makes seeds?

○ roots   ○ flowers   ○ stems

6. All plants have _____.

○ flowers   ○ cones   ○ life cycles

7. Where do people grow plants to eat?

○ zoo   ○ garden   ○ store

8. A new plant grows from a _____.

○ seed   ○ spine   ○ leaf

9. Which is a part of a plant's life cycle?

○ spine   ○ seedling   ○ stem

10. Plants give off oxygen through their _____.

○ leaves   ○ stems   ○ roots

Chapter 2
Animals

wings
fins
mammal
lungs
gills
reptile
amphibian
adult

fins

Fins are body parts that help a fish move.

mammal

A mammal is an animal whose mother makes milk to feed her babies.

reptile

A reptile is an animal that has dry skin with scales.

adult

An adult is a full-grown plant, animal, or person.

How Do Animals Use Their Parts?

Science and You

A lizard uses its tail and legs like you use your hands.

Inquiry Skill

Infer Use what you know and what you observe to tell what you think.

 STANDARDS
SC.H.1.1.3.1.1. works with others to complete an experiment or to solve a problem.

What You Need

backgrounds

animal cutouts

crayons

glue

Hidden Animals

Steps

STEP 1

1. **Observe** Look at a background. Color an animal so that it looks like the background.

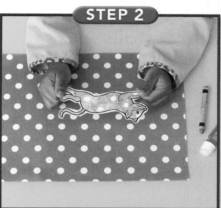

STEP 2

2. Glue your animal on the background to hide it.

3. **Compare** Trade pictures with a classmate. Try to find the hidden animal.

STEP 3

Think and Share

1. Why was the paper animal able to hide on the background?

2. **Infer** Tell how you think an animal's body color helps it hide outside.

Investigate More!

Ask Questions How might an animal's body shape help it hide? Finish this question. How does a _____'s body shape help it hide?

A31

Reading Skill
Main Idea and Details

STANDARDS
SC.F.1.1.4.1.1. knows that plants and animals have adaptations that help them survive in their environment (camouflage, teeth, spines).
SC.F.2.1.2.1.3. knows some ways in which animals and plants are adapted to living in different environments.

Animal Body Parts

Animals have body parts that help them find food and stay safe. Animals use their eyes, ears, noses, legs, tails, and other parts to help them live.

Bush Baby

Large eyes help it see at night.

Ears help it find insects to eat.

Gray fur helps it hide in trees.

Legs and fingers help it catch food and hold onto trees.

Some animals can use body parts to hurt other animals or scare them away. Some animals have colors or shapes that help them hide.

Using Body Parts to Stay Safe

quills

stinger

claws and teeth

smell

sound

color and shape

▶ **MAIN IDEA** What body parts help animals find food?

Parts for Moving

Animals have body parts that help them move. A bird has **wings** that help it fly through the air. A bird also has legs that help it walk, hop, and hold on to trees.

A fish has a tail and **fins** that help it move. A lion has strong legs that help it run and climb.

▶ **MAIN IDEA** How does a bird use its legs?

tail

fin

leg

wing

Lesson Wrap-Up

1. **Vocabulary** How do **fins** help a fish?

2. **Reading Skill** What are some ways in which body parts help animals?

3. **Infer** How does body color help an animal stay safe?

Technology Visit **www.eduplace.com/scp/** to find out more about animal body parts.

Read to find out about the snowshoe hare in winter and in summer.

In a Winter Meadow

by Jack Prelutsky

In a winter meadow
icy breezes blow,
snowshoe hares are running
softly through the snow.

Up and down they scurry,
darting left and right,
snowshoe hares are running,
dressed in winter white.

STANDARDS
SC.F.1.1.4.1.1. knows that plants and animals have adaptations that help them survive in their environment (camouflage, teeth, spines).

READING LINK

Animal Disguises
by Belinda Weber

Kingfisher Young Knowledge
Animal Disguises

Snowshoe hares live in Alaska. In the summer their coats are brown in order to blend in with the ground. In the winter the hares grow new, white coats to help them stay hidden in the snow.

Sharing Ideas

1. **Write About It** How are snowshoe hares protected in winter?

2. **Talk About It** Why does the snowshoe hare's color change in summer?

How Are Animals Grouped?

Science and You

The birds, turtles, and squirrels you see in a park are in different animal groups.

Inquiry Skill

Classify Group objects that are alike in some way.

STANDARDS
SC.H.1.1.4.1.1. uses simple graphs, pictures, written statements, and numbers to observe, describe, record, and compare data.

What You Need

animal pictures

graph paper

crayons

Classify Animals

Steps

1. **Classify** Sort animal pictures into groups that are alike in some way.

STEP 1

2. **Record Data** Make a graph to show your groups. Label each group. Color in one block on your graph for every animal.

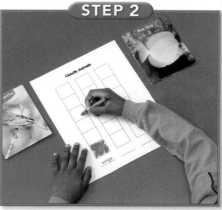
STEP 2

3. **Communicate** Tell how you sorted the animals. Tell how many animals are in each group.

STEP 3

Think and Share

1. How are the animals in a group alike?

2. How can you use body parts to group animals?

Investigate More!

Solve a Problem Suppose you have a friend who has never seen a turtle. How would you tell your friend what a turtle looks like?

▶ **Vocabulary**

mammal
lungs
gills
reptile
amphibian

▶ **Reading Skill**
Compare and Contrast

STANDARDS
SC.F.1.1.5.1.1. understands different ways in which living things can be grouped (for example, plant/animals, edible plants/non-edible plants).
SC.G.1.1.2.1.2. understands that animals can be grouped according to what they eat.

Mammals

Some scientists study how animals are alike and different. They group animals that have like body parts.

One group of animals is called mammals. A **mammal** is an animal whose mother makes milk to feed her babies. Most mammals have hair or fur. They have **lungs**, or body parts that take in air.

Birds and Fish

Birds and fish do not have all the same body parts that mammals have. Birds have wings to fly. A bird's body is covered with feathers. Birds have mouth parts called bills.

▲ A bird uses lungs to breathe.

A fish lives in water. **Gills** are the parts of a fish that help it breathe underwater.

▶ **COMPARE AND CONTRAST**
What body parts do mammals, birds, and fish use to breathe?

Most fish have bodies covered with scales.

scales

gills

Reptiles and Amphibians

Reptiles and amphibians look different from mammals and birds. A **reptile** is an animal that has dry skin with scales. It has lungs for breathing. Snakes, lizards, and turtles are reptiles.

An **amphibian** is an animal that has wet skin with no hair, feathers, or scales. It spends some time in water and some time on land. Frogs, toads, and salamanders are amphibians.

What Animals Eat

You can group animals by what they eat. Some animals eat plants. Some eat other animals. Some animals eat plants and animals.

Animals that eat other animals have sharp teeth.

Animals that only eat plants have flat teeth.

▶ **COMPARE AND CONTRAST** How are the teeth of animals different?

Lesson Wrap-Up

❶ **Vocabulary** What are **gills**?

❷ **Reading Skill** How are fish and reptiles alike?

❸ **Classify** Which animal is an amphibian—a snake, a frog, or a fish?

Technology Visit **www.eduplace.com/scp/** to find out more about animal groups.

How Do Animals Grow and Change?

Science and You

A tiny kitten grows up to be an adult cat.

Inquiry Skill

Use Models Use pictures to learn about real objects.

 STANDARDS
SC.H.1.1.4.1.1. uses simple graphs, pictures, written statements, and numbers to observe, describe, record, and compare data.

What You Need

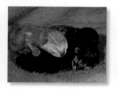

cat pictures

A Cat's Life Cycle

Steps

STEP 1

1. **Observe** Look at pictures of a growing cat. See how the pictures are different.

STEP 2

2. **Use Models** Order the cat pictures from youngest to oldest.

3. **Communicate** Use the pictures to tell a friend about a cat's life cycle.

STEP 3

Think and Share

1. Which picture shows the youngest cat?

2. **Compare** How does the cat look different in the first and last pictures?

Investigate More!

Ask Questions What else do you want to know about how an animal grows? Find someone to help you get an answer. Share what you learn.

STANDARDS

SC.F.1.1.3.1.2. knows that living things grow and change in different ways and in different lengths of time (for example, butterfly, frog, daisy, pine tree).
SC.F.2.1.1.1.1. knows that plants and animals are similar but not identical to their parents.

Animal Life Cycles

Animals go through changes called a life cycle. First, an animal is born or hatches from an egg. Then it grows to be an adult. An **adult** is a full-grown plant, animal, or person. A life cycle begins again when an adult animal has babies.

Life Cycle of a Salamander

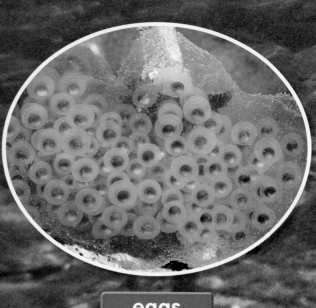

eggs

ready to hatch

Some animals grow faster than others. Salamanders become adults in about 3 months. Elephants take 20 years to grow up.

▶ **SEQUENCE** **What part of a salamander's life cycle comes after the adult?**

growing

adult

Parents and Young Animals

Adult animals can become parents of baby animals. Some young animals look like their parents when they are born. A puppy looks like its parents. A frog does not look like its parents until it is an adult.

These puppies do not look exactly like their mother. ▶

Lesson Wrap-Up

❶ Vocabulary What is an **adult**?

❷ Reading Skill How does an animal's life cycle begin?

❸ Use Models How can pictures help you understand an animal's life cycle?

Technology Visit **www.eduplace.com/scp/** to find out more about animal life cycles.

LINKS
for Home and School

Math Story Problems

Jane took a walk. She saw birds, bees, cats, and worms.

1. How many animals with wings did Jane see?

2. Use the chart. Write an animal story problem. Then solve a partner's story problem.

Animals on My Walk	
Animal	Tally
🐦	‖‖‖
🐝	‖‖‖
🐱	‖‖‖
🪱	‖

Language Arts Animal Names

The words below are names for groups of animals. Draw a picture of a group. Then write a sentence about your picture.

A female cat has a kindle of kittens.

gaggle of geese   **pride of lions**

kindle of kittens   **swarm of bees**

pod of whales   **herd of elephants**

school of fish

Visual Summary

There are different kinds of animals.
They grow in different ways.

Kinds of Animals				
Mammal	**Bird**	**Fish**	**Reptile**	**Amphibian**

Main Ideas

1. How does a fish move? (p. A34)

2. How can you use teeth to group animals? (p. A43)

3. What is a full-grown animal called? (p. A46)

4. How are animal life cycles different? (p. A47)

SAT 10 Practice

Vocabulary and Science Skills

Choose the correct answer.

5. Which helps a bush baby hide in trees?

○ ears   ○ fur   ○ eyes

6. Which help fish breathe?

○ gills   ○ scales   ○ fins

7. Which has dry skin and scales?

○ mammal   ○ bird   ○ reptile

8. Which lives in water and on land?

○ frog   ○ lion   ○ owl

9. Which body parts help a bird move?

○ ears   ○ teeth   ○ wings

10. Animals that only eat plants have _____.

○ sharp teeth   ○ flat teeth   ○ long teeth

Chapter 3

People

senses
infant
teen
exercise
sleep

senses

Your senses help you see, hear, smell, taste, and feel things.

infant

A new baby is called an infant.

teen

A teen is a person between 13 and 19 years old.

exercise

Exercise is movement that keeps your body strong.

How Do People Use Their Parts?

Science and You

Your body has parts that help you move and do other things.

Inquiry Skill

Communicate Share with others what you learn and observe.

STANDARDS
SC.H.1.1.3.1.1. works with others to complete an experiment or to solve a problem.

What You Need

paper

NON-TOXIC CRAYONS
CRAYONS
WASHABLE CRAYONS
8 PIECES

crayons

Model Your Body

Steps

1. Draw a picture of yourself.

2. **Use Models** Draw a line to each body part on your picture. Label each part.

3. **Communicate** Share your picture with a partner. Name each body part, and tell what it does.

STEP 1

STEP 2

leg

Think and Share

1. How did your hands help you with the picture?

2. Pick one body part that you drew. Tell what it does.

STEP 3

head

hand

leg

eye

arm

Investigate More!

Experiment You hear with your ears. Close your eyes for one minute. Listen. Then list what you heard.

► **Vocabulary**

senses

► **Reading Skill**
Draw
Conclusions

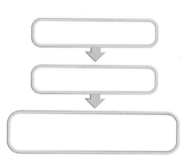

Your Senses

You have **senses** that help you feel, smell, hear, see, and taste things. Different body parts are used for each sense. Your senses help keep you safe. They also help you learn about the world.

▶ **DRAW CONCLUSIONS** How do you think popcorn feels, looks, and sounds?

You use your hands to feel.

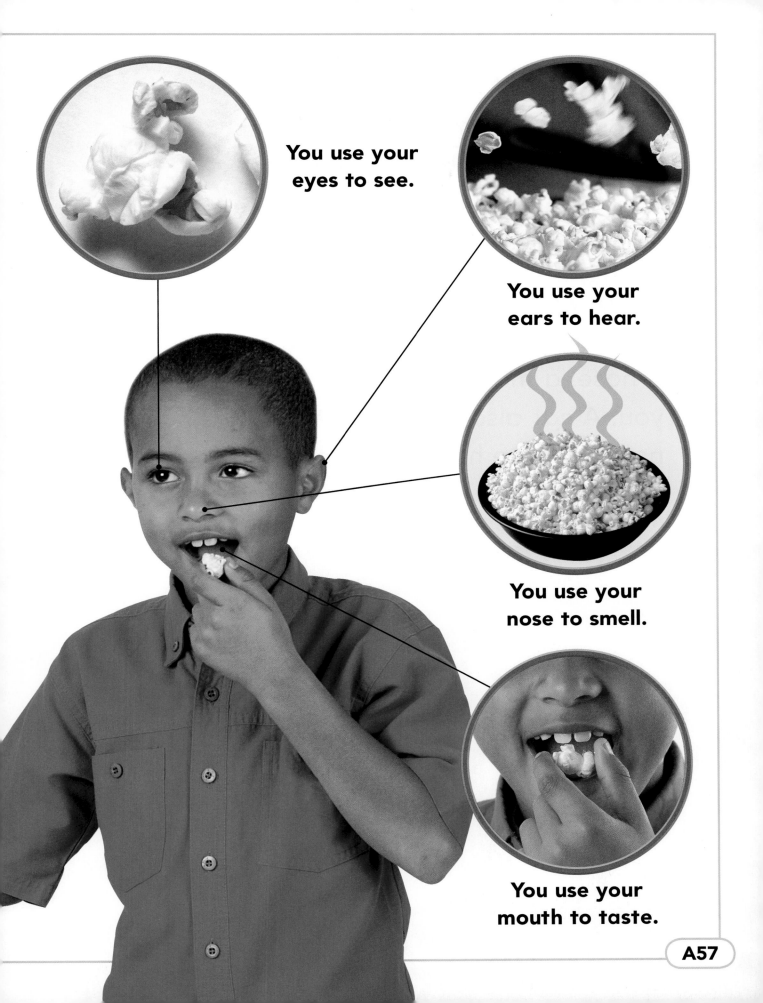

You use your
eyes to see.

You use your
ears to hear.

You use your
nose to smell.

You use your
mouth to taste.

Other Body Parts

Your body parts work together to help you do things. You use your arms and legs to ride a bike. Hands and arms help you draw.

Many animals have body parts like yours. A cat has eyes, ears, a nose, a mouth, and legs. So do you. A cat also has paws. You do not. You have hands and feet.

mouth to talk and eat

▲ arms and hands to hold

legs to walk and run ▶

 **DRAW CONCLUSIONS** What body parts help you play on a playground?

Lesson Wrap-Up

❶ **Vocabulary** How do your **senses** help you?

❷ **Reading Skill** How do people and lions use their legs?

❸ **Communicate** How can you share what you know about people's body parts?

Technology Visit **www.eduplace.com/scp/** to find out more about your body parts.

Florida Activity Trails

To have a healthy body, you need to put your body parts to work! Florida's warm, sunny weather makes it easy to be active outdoors.

In north Florida, there are many springs. Some bike trails go from one spring to another. You can swim in one of the springs.

Ichetucknee Springs State Park

STANDARDS
SC.B.1.1.4.1.1. knows ways that human activities require and release energy.

Bok Tower Gardens

You can play ball or fly kites in some of Florida's parks. You can ride your bike, walk, or skate on some of the trails.

Sharing Ideas

1. **Write About It** Write about different ways that you moved your body today.

2. **Talk About It** Talk with a partner. Tell three ways that you can add more activity to your day.

How Do People Grow and Change?

Science and You

You will keep growing until you are an adult.

Inquiry Skill

Work Together Share what you observe with a partner.

STANDARDS
SC.H.1.1.5.1.2. uses standard (for example, centimeters) and nonstandard units (for example, paper clips, hands, pencils) to measure organisms and objects and parts of organisms and objects.

What You Need

pictures

A Person's Life

Steps

1. **Observe** Look at pictures of a person.

2. **Compare** Order the pictures to show how the person changed as she grew.

3. **Communicate** Tell a partner how the pictures show the changes in the life cycle of a person.

STEP 1

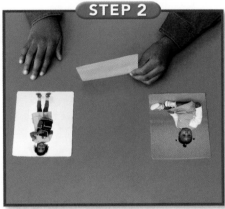
STEP 2

STEP 3

Think and Share

1. What is the beginning of a person's life?

2. **Infer** What is one way that a person changes as he or she grows?

Investigate More!

Work Together Spread out your hand. Have a friend measure from your little finger to your thumb. Then measure an adult's hand. Share what you learn.

▶ **Vocabulary**

infant

teen

exercise

sleep

▶ **Reading Skill**

Sequence

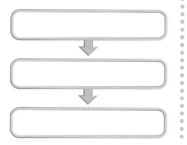

People Grow and Change

People grow and change all through their lives. You were an **infant**, or baby, when you were born. Then you grew and learned to walk and talk. You kept growing and started going to school. All this time, your family took care of you. They helped you learn new things.

school-age child

toddler

infant

You will grow to be a teen. A **teen** is a person between 13 and 19 years old. Next, you will become an adult.

You will take care of yourself when you are an adult. Your body will stop growing taller.

▶ **SEQUENCE** When will you become a teen?

teen

adult

senior adult

Eat and Exercise for Health

You need to eat and exercise to stay healthy. Food gives you energy to live and grow. Things like fruits, vegetables, and milk help your body grow strong.

Foods to Eat

Eat More of These Foods	Eat Less of These Foods

Exercise is movement that keeps your body strong. Running and jumping make your bones and muscles strong. They also make your lungs and heart strong.

▶ **DRAW CONCLUSIONS** Why do you need to exercise?

How are these children exercising?

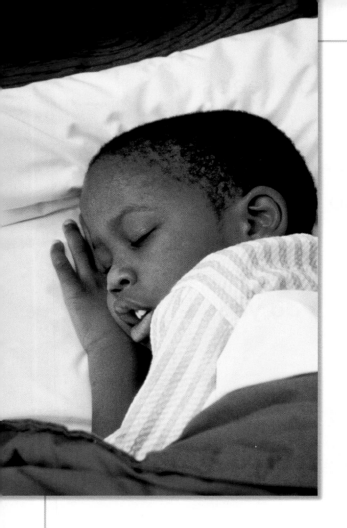

Get Enough Sleep

People need sleep. You rest your body and mind when you **sleep**. A good night's sleep will help you stay healthy and have lots of energy. Children in first grade need about ten hours of sleep each night.

Lesson Wrap-Up

❶ **Vocabulary** What is one kind of **exercise**?

❷ **Reading Skill** What do people grow to be after they are teens?

❸ **Work Together** Talk to a friend about how an infant is different from an adult.

Technology Visit **www.eduplace.com/scp/** to find out more about people growing and changing.

Math **Make a Pictograph**

Look at the chart of children's favorite fruits.

Mr. William's Class	
Favorite Fruit	Tally
🍎 apple	|||
🍇 grapes	||||
🍌 banana	||
🍉 watermelon		

Make a picture graph to show the data from the chart in a different way.

Social Studies **World Foods**

Americans eat many foods that are popular in other countries. People in Mexico like tamales. Pasta is a favorite in Italy. Fried bananas are treats in Africa. Write about your family's favorite foods.

My family likes tacos.

Visual Summary

People are living things that have needs.

Healthful Habits

| Food | Exercise | Sleep |

Main Ideas

1. What do your senses do? **(p. A56)**

2. For which of the senses do you use your nose? **(p. A57)**

3. What does food do for you? **(p. A66)**

4. How much sleep does a first-grader need? **(p. A68)**

Vocabulary and Science Skills

Choose the correct answer.

5. Which gives your body rest?

○ senses   ○ exercise   ○ sleep

6. Which do you use to smell?

○ eyes   ○ nose   ○ mouth

7. When you are born, you are _____.

○ an adult   ○ a teen   ○ an infant

8. Exercise keeps your body _____.

○ tall   ○ strong   ○ rested

9. Food gives you _____.

○ energy   ○ exercise   ○ sleep

10. Which body part is most like a cat's paws?

○ legs   ○ feet   ○ arms

Discover!

What bird flaps its wings the fastest?

A hummingbird flaps its wings about 75 times every second! The wings move so fast that they make a humming sound. Hummingbirds are called nature's helicopters because of the way they move.

Go to **www.eduplace.com/scp/** to learn more about the parts of a hummingbird.

LIFE  SCIENCE

UNIT B

Living Things and Where They Live

Cricket Connection

Visit www.eduplace.com/scp/ to check out *Click, Ask,* and *Odyssey* magazine articles and activities.

Coastal Wildlife of Florida

Ghost Crab

Lives: sandy Atlantic beaches

Eats: sand fleas

Lifespan: up to 3 years

Fun fact: it runs sideways

American Crocodile

Lives: south Florida

Eats: crabs, fish, small mammals, water birds

Lifespan: 50 to 60 years

Fun fact: 500 to 1,200 live in Florida

Schaus Swallowtail Butterfly

Lives: Florida Keys

Eats: nectar of guava blossoms

Lifespan: 1 month as adult

Fun fact: can fly up to 3.6 miles a day

Queen Conch

Lives: south Florida and the Keys

Eats: algae, dead material, sea grasses

Lifespan: 20 to 30 years

Fun fact: full size is 12 inches long, 5 pounds

LIFE **UNIT B** SCIENCE

Living Things and Where They Live

Reading in Science............. **B2**

Chapter 4
Living Things **B4**

Chapter 5
Where Plants and
Animals Live..................... **B24**

Independent Reading

Living Things

First Lady of the Sea

Desert Life

Discover!

Why do you find shells on the beach?

Think about this question as you read. You will have the answer by the end of the unit.

Over in the Meadow

illustrated by Ezra Jack Keats

Over in the meadow
    where the stream runs blue,
Lived an old mother fish,
    and her little fishes two.
"Swim!" said the mother.
    "We swim," said the two.
So they swam and they leaped,
    Where the stream runs blue.

Chapter 4

Living Things

living thing

nonliving thing

food

sunlight

shelter

living thing

A living thing grows, changes, and makes other living things like itself.

nonliving thing

A nonliving thing does not eat, drink, grow, and make other things like itself.

food

Food is what living things use to get energy.

shelter

Shelter is a safe place for animals to live.

What Is a Living Thing?

Science and You

You and your pets are living things.

Inquiry Skill

Classify Group objects that are alike in some way.

STANDARDS
SC.H.1.1.4.1.1. uses simple graphs, pictures, written sentences and numbers to observe, describe, record, and compare data.

objects

crayons and paper

Classify Objects

Steps

STEP 1

1. **Observe** Look for ways in which some objects are alike or different.

2. **Classify** Sort the objects into groups that are alike in one way.

STEP 2

3. **Record Data** Draw a picture of the objects in each group. Write the names of your groups.

Think and Share

STEP 3

1. How are the objects in each group alike?

2. **Compare** How do your groups compare to those of the rest of the class?

Investigate More!

Work Together Cut out pictures of objects from magazines. Talk with a partner about a rule for sorting the objects. Then use the rule.

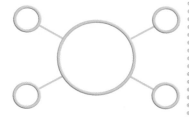

Living Things

A **living thing** grows, changes, and makes other living things like itself. It needs air, food, water, and space to stay alive.

People, birds, and squirrels are living things. Flowers, trees, and grass are living things, too. They all grow and change. They can make more living things like themselves.

► **MAIN IDEA** What does a living thing do?

The squirrel is a living thing.

The children, the trees, and
the grass are living things.

Nonliving Things

A **nonliving thing** does not eat, drink, grow, and make other things like itself. It does not need food, water, and air. Rocks, bikes, and clothes are all nonliving things.

◄ living things

◄ nonliving thing

The girl is a living thing.
The doll is a nonliving thing.

Some nonliving things may act like living things. A fire grows. A fire needs air to burn. It takes up space. But fire does not need food or water. A fire is a nonliving thing.

▶ **MAIN IDEA** What is a nonliving thing?

fire

Lesson Wrap-Up

❶ **Vocabulary** What is a **living thing**?

❷ **Reading Skill** Name three nonliving things.

❸ **Classify** Is water a living thing or a nonliving thing? Explain your answer.

💻 **Technology** Visit **www.eduplace.com/scp/** to find out more about living and nonliving things.

Living or Nonliving?

Cast   **Mr. Chen:** teacher
Emma: student
Peter: student

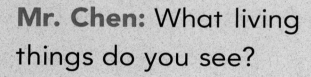

Mr. Chen: What living things do you see?

Emma: I see baby rabbits. They will grow and change.

STANDARDS
SC.F.1.1.1.1.1. understands that living things need food, water, space, and shelter to survive.

READING **LINK**

Peter: I see a goat drinking water from a pail. The goat is living. The pail and the water are not.

Mr. Chen: Right! How do you know?

Peter: Well, the goat needs water and air. That means it is living.

Emma: The goat also needs food and space to grow. The pail does not need those things.

Mr. Chen: Maybe all living things need nonliving things.

Emma: I am a living thing that needs a nonliving thing. I need lunch!

Sharing Ideas

1. **Write About It** Write a story about the living and nonliving things in a park.

2. **Talk About It** What are some nonliving things that it would be difficult to live without?

What Do Living Things Need?

Science and You

Knowing the needs of living things helps you take care of them.

Inquiry Skill

Observe Use your senses to find out about objects.

STANDARDS
SC.B.1.1.3.1.1. understands that models (for example, terrarium or aquarium) can be used to observe processes and changes over time.

What You Need

goggles

terrarium supplies

plants

water

Observe Plants

Steps

STEP 1

1. **Safety:** Wear goggles! Use gravel, soil, and plants to make a terrarium like the one in the picture.

2. Spray a little water on the soil.

STEP 2

3. Cover the terrarium. Put the terrarium in a sunny place. **Safety:** Wash your hands after you finish!

4. **Observe** Look at the plants every day for one week. Record what you see.

STEP 3

Think and Share

1. **Infer** Are the plants living things? How do you know?

2. What do plants need?

Investigate More!

Ask Questions How much light do your plants need? Finish this question: What would happen to the plants if I _____? Make a plan for finding an answer.

Vocabulary

food

sunlight

shelter

Reading Skill

Categorize and Classify

STANDARDS

SC.F.1.1.1.1.1. understands that living things need food, water, space, and shelter to survive.

SC.G.1.1.2.1.3. understands that living things are part of a food chain.

Food

Food is what living things use to get energy. Plants and animals need food.

Plants use sunlight, air, and water to make their own food. **Sunlight** is energy from the Sun. Most plants die if they do not get sunlight.

These cows are eating plants.

Animals eat food when they are hungry. Some animals eat plants. Some animals eat other animals. Many animals eat both plants and animals. Most people eat both plants and animals.

▶ **CLASSIFY** How do plants get food?

▲ **This heron is eating a fish.**

Food Chain

Plants use sunlight, air, and water to make food.

An insect eats plants.

A bird eats insects.

Water, Air, and Space

Plants and animals need water, air, and space to live. Most plants get water from the ground. Many animals get water by drinking. Some animals get water from the food they eat.

How are the giraffes getting what they need?

Plants need water to live.

Living things need air and space to live and grow. Plants use air to help them make food. Animals breathe in air.

Plants need space so that they can get the sunlight and water they need. Animals need space so that they can find food and homes.

▶ **CLASSIFY** How do animals get water?

Plants need space to grow.

Whales breathe air just as you do.

Shelter

Animals need shelter. **Shelter** is a safe place for animals to live. Animals find shelter in trees, in mud, and under the ground. Some animals even find shelter on other animals.

shelter in the ground

shelter on another animal

Lesson Wrap-Up

❶ **Vocabulary** What kinds of **food** do animals eat?

❷ **Reading Skill** What do plants need to live?

❸ **Observe** Look at the picture. What need is the child taking care of?

Technology Visit **www.eduplace. com/scp/** to find out more about the needs of living things.

LINKS for Home and School

Math Measure Living Things

Use a ruler to measure a plant. Record your data in a table. Measure again every month. Tell how much the plant grew.

Measurements of My Plants	
Date	Measurement
October 1	3 inches
November 1	4 inches
December 1	$4\frac{1}{2}$ inches
January 1	5 inches
February 1	6 inches

Social Studies Where People Live

Draw a picture of a place where people live. Write a sentence to tell how the place meets people's needs.

It keeps people warm.

Visual Summary

The world is made of living and nonliving things.

Living Thing	Nonliving Thing
• grows and changes • makes other living things like itself • needs food, water, air, and space	• does not eat, drink and grow • does not make other things like itself • does not need food, water, and air

Main Ideas

1. What do all living things need? (p. B8)

2. How are nonliving things different from living things? (p. B10)

3. How do plants use sunlight? (pp. B16–B17)

4. Where do most plants get water? (p. B18)

Vocabulary and Science Skills

Choose the correct answer.

5. A living thing needs _____.
   ○ trees   ○ fire   ○ water

6. Plants need sunlight to make _____.
   ○ food   ○ space   ○ seeds

7. Which is a nonliving thing?
   ○ flower   ○ book   ○ bird

8. A safe place for animals is _____.
   ○ a shelter   ○ a park   ○ a street

9. All living things _____.
   ○ sleep   ○ grow   ○ run

10. Shelter for a fox might be in _____.
   ○ the ground   ○ a pond
   ○ some mud

Chapter 5

Where Plants and Animals Live

forest
ocean
wetland
desert

forest

A forest is a place with many trees that grow close together.

ocean

An ocean is a large body of salty water.

wetland

A wetland is a low area of land that is very wet.

desert

A desert is a place with very little water.

What Lives in Forests?

Science and You

You save the home of many living things when you protect a tree.

Inquiry Skill

Communicate Share information with others.

STANDARDS
SC.H.1.1.5.1.1. uses a variety of tools (for example, thermometers, magnifiers, rulers, scales, computers) to identify characteristics of objects.

What You Need

hand lens

crayons

paper

Observe a Tree

Steps

1. **Observe** Go outside. Use a hand lens to look closely at the parts of a tree.

STEP 1

2. **Record Data** Make a list of living things you find. Then draw a tree. Show the living things that you found.

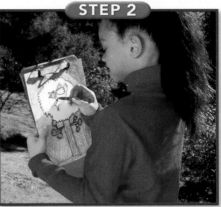
STEP 2

3. **Communicate** Talk about your drawing with a partner. Find out if you saw different things.

STEP 3

Think and Share

1. What did you find on and under the tree?

2. **Infer** How do trees help the living things you saw?

Investigate More!

Work Together Work with a partner. Talk about what should be in a forest. Choose the best ideas. Then make a model of a forest in a shoebox.

**What are some
living and nonliving
things in the forest?**

A Forest

A **forest** is a place with many trees that grow close together. Forest animals live in trees, bushes, or on the forest floor. Animals use the living and nonliving things in a forest for food and shelter.

▶ **MAIN IDEA** What is a forest?

bear

snake

katydid

blue jay

owl

squirrel

beetle

deer

raccoon

earthworm

lizard

turtle

B29

Other Kinds of Forests

There are many kinds of forests. Some forests are hot and rainy. Others are cold and dry. There are different kinds of plants and animals in each kind of forest.

▶ **MAIN IDEA** How are forests different from one another?

▲ great horned owl

bobcat ▶

A pine forest can be warm or cold. It is not as wet as a rain forest.

It is warm and rainy in a tropical rain forest.

parrot ▶

Lesson Wrap-Up

❶ **Vocabulary** What do you call a place that has many trees close together?

❷ **Reading Skill** Are all forests the same? Tell why or why not.

❸ **Communicate** Tell a partner what a tropical rain forest is like.

Technology Visit **www.eduplace.com/scp/** to find out more about forests.

What Lives in Oceans and Wetlands?

Science and You

You can have fun playing in the ocean, but it is also a home for many living things.

Inquiry Skill

Compare Tell how objects or events are alike or different.

animal pictures

STANDARDS
SC.H.1.1.4.1.1. uses simple graphs, pictures, written statements, and numbers to observe, describe, record, and compare data.

Compare Animals

Steps

1. **Compare** Look at animal pictures. Tell how animals are alike and different.

2. **Classify** Sort the animal pictures into groups that are alike in one way.

3. Name your groups. Make a list of the animals in each group.

STEP 1

STEP 2

STEP 3

Think and Share

1. **Compare** Tell what is alike about the animals in each group. Tell how the groups are different.

2. What body parts do you think help these animals live where they do?

Investigate More!

Ask Questions Make a list of things you want to learn about one animal. Write each thing as a question. Make a plan to answer your questions.

▶ **Vocabulary**

ocean

wetland

▶ **Reading Skill**

Compare and
Contrast

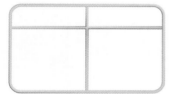

The Ocean

An **ocean** is a large body of salty water. Oceans are nonliving things, but they have many living things in them. Some animals live on land but eat ocean animals. Other animals live in the air and water near the shore. Many animals live in deep water.

What are some living and nonliving things in the ocean?

whale

jellyfish

manta

Ocean animals have parts that help them stay alive in water. Fish have fins and tails to swim. They have gills to breathe air. Some animals have colors that help them hide.

▶ **COMPARE AND CONTRAST** What are some ways in which fish are alike?

gull

dolphin

shark

turtle

crab

A Wetland

A **wetland** is a low area of land that is very wet. The water in a wetland can be salty or not salty.

Many kinds of plants and animals live in wetlands. Wetland animals find food, water, and shelter in the mud, water, and plants.

▶ **COMPARE AND CONTRAST** What are two different kinds of wetlands?

snail

snake

heron

dragonfly

alligator

hawk

panther

muskrat

mosquito

stork

Lesson Wrap-Up

❶ **Vocabulary** What is a large body of salty water called?

❷ **Reading Skill** How are oceans different from wetlands?

❸ **Compare** How are oceans like wetlands?

Technology Visit **www.eduplace.com/scp/** to find out more about oceans and wetlands.

Marjory Stoneman Douglas

Writer and Environmentalist

Marjory Douglas worried about the Everglades. The Everglades is a Florida wetland.

People wanted to build homes, stores, and roads in the Everglades. Douglas knew that would cause many plants and animals to die. So she wrote books and stories to tell why the Everglades should be saved.

Her work paid off. Today the Everglades is a national park. It will be protected forever.

STANDARDS
SC.D.2.1.1.1.1. extends and refines knowledge of ways to care for the Earth at home and in school.

SOCIAL STUDIES **LINK**

sawgrass

purple gallinule

Sharing Ideas

1. **Write About It** Why did Douglas worry about the Everglades?

2. **Talk About It** Use your own words to tell why people remember Marjory Stoneman Douglas.

What Lives in a Desert?

Science and You

You need to drink a lot of water when you are in a desert.

Inquiry Skill

Use Numbers You can count to know the right amount each time.

STANDARDS
SC.H.1.1.2.1.1. understands the importance of accuracy and repetition in conducting scientific inquiries.

What You Need

dry sponges

wax paper

dropper and water

plate

Wet or Dry

Steps

1. **Use Numbers** Squeeze four droppers full of water onto a sponge. Put four droppers of water on the other sponge.

2. Wrap wax paper all around one sponge. Do not wrap the other sponge.

3. **Compare** Put the sponges on a plate. Wait one day. Touch the sponges. How are they different?

STEP 1

STEP 2

STEP 3

Think and Share

1. Which sponge was wetter?

2. **Infer** What can you say about the wax paper and water?

Investigate More!

Experiment Repeat the experiment two more times exactly the same way. What happens? What does this tell you about science experiments?

Vocabulary

desert

Reading Skill
Draw Conclusions

STANDARDS
SC.F.1.1.4.1.1. knows that plants and animals
have adaptations that help them survive in their
environment.

The Desert

A **desert** is a place with very little water. The air can be hot or cold. The ground in a hot desert is mostly covered with rocks or sand.

Living in a desert is not easy. It can be hard to find food and water in such a dry place.

prickly pear

jackrabbit

lizard

rat

What are some living and nonliving things in the desert?

The air is hot in this desert. Many animals hide or sleep during the day. They look for food at night when the air is cool.

▶ **DRAW CONCLUSIONS** Why do many desert animals sleep during the day?

fox

snake

saguaro

scorpion

Living in Deserts

Desert plants and animals have parts that help them live in dry places. A cactus has thick stems and waxy skin that hold water. A kangaroo rat's body makes water from the seeds it eats.

A camel has wide feet that help it walk in sand. ▶

Lesson Wrap-Up

❶ **Vocabulary** What is a place with very little water called?

❷ **Reading Skill** Why do many desert plants have waxy skin?

❸ **Use Numbers** How can you use numbers to help you do a science experiment?

Technology Visit **www.eduplace.com/scp/** to find out more about deserts.

LINKS for Home and School

Math Make a Counting Book

Make a counting book. On the first page, draw one living thing. Write the number 1 on the page. Make seven more pages. Add one living thing each time.

1. How many things are on your last page?

2. How many more things are on the third page than the first page?

Language Arts What If?

What if the whole world was a wetland? What if animals only lived in deserts? Think of a "what if" question. Then write a story to answer the question.

Visual Summary

Living things are found in many places.

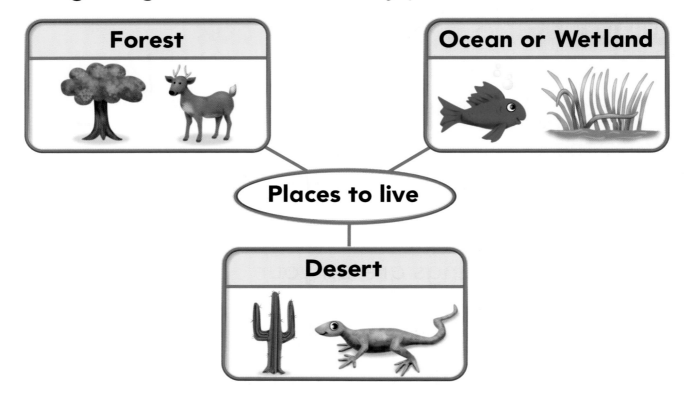

Forest

Ocean or Wetland

Places to live

Desert

Main Ideas

1. What are two kinds of forests? **(pp. B30–B31)**

2. Name three animals that live in an ocean. **(pp. B34–B35)**

3. Where do wetland animals find food, water, and shelter? **(p. B36)**

4. What helps a cactus hold water? **(p. B44)**

Vocabulary and Science Skills

Choose the correct answer.

5. Many trees grow in _____.

○ a desert   ○ a forest   ○ an ocean

6. Where might alligators live?

○ a desert   ○ a forest   ○ a wetland

7. Which lives in an ocean?

○ whale   ○ rabbit   ○ bear

8. Deserts have only a little _____.

○ sand   ○ water   ○ air

9. A desert cactus holds water in its _____.

○ stem   ○ flowers   ○ spines

10. Which helps fish swim in oceans?

○ sand   ○ colors   ○ fins

Discover!

Why do you find shells on the beach?

Some ocean animals are covered with a hard shell. The hard shell protects the animal's soft body. After the animal dies, the shell is empty. Waves push the empty shell onto the beach.

Go to **www.eduplace.com/scp/** to visit the underwater world of shells.

Earth, Our Home

Famous Crops of Florida

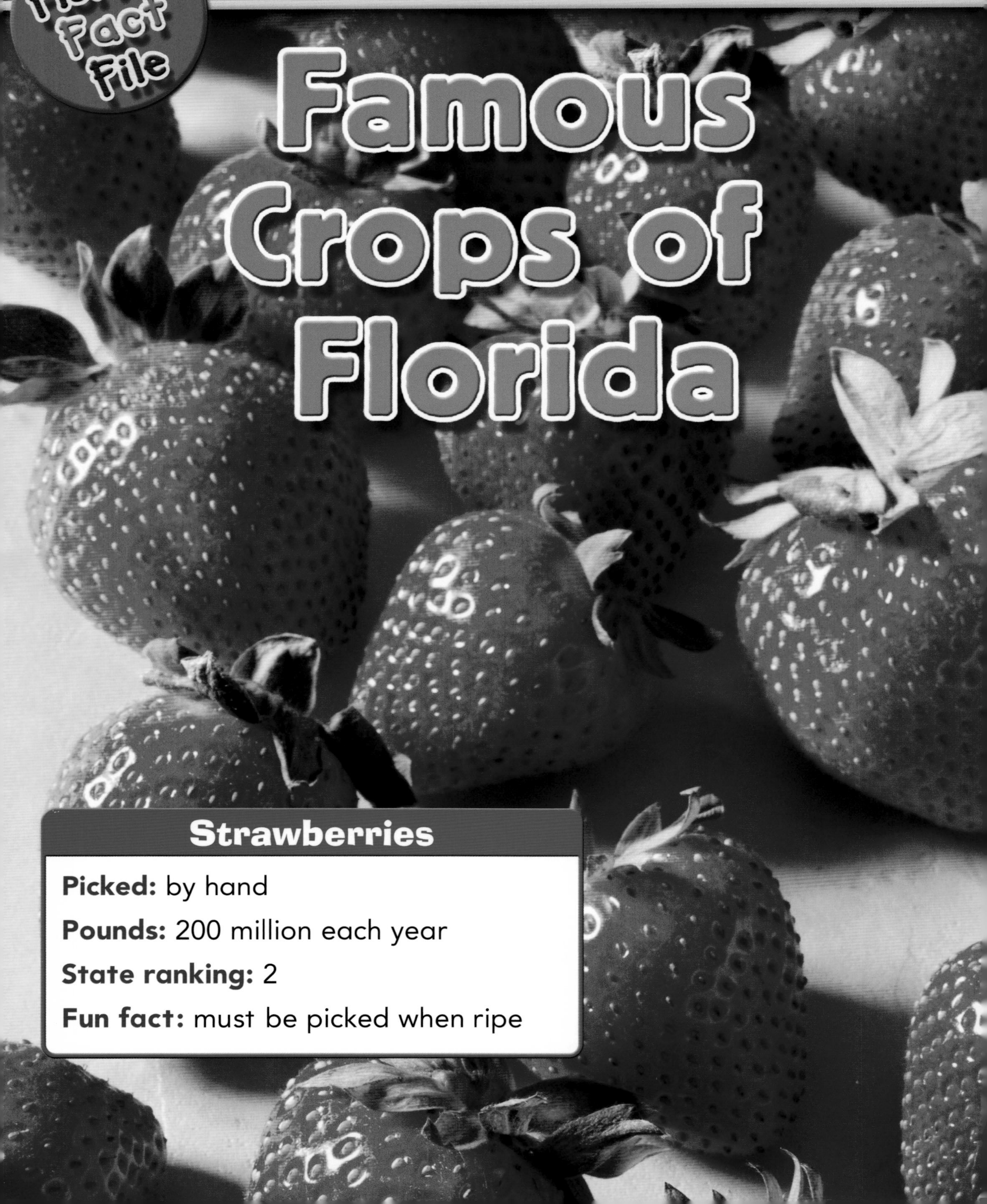

Strawberries

Picked: by hand

Pounds: 200 million each year

State ranking: 2

Fun fact: must be picked when ripe

Oranges

Picked: by hand

Boxes: 242 million each year

State ranking: 1

Fun fact: 2½ oranges make one cup of juice

Grapefruit

Picked: by hand

Boxes: 41 million each year

State ranking: 1

Fun fact: trees live to be 25 years old

Avocados

Picked: by hand

Baskets: 660,612 each year

State ranking: 2

Fun fact: trees live at least 50 years

Earth, Our Home

Reading in Science.............. **C2**

Chapter 6
Looking at Our Earth **C4**

Chapter 7
Caring for Our Earth **C30**

Independent Reading

7 Uses for Air

What Makes a Garden Grow

We Can Recycle

Discover!

Why do rocks have different colors?

Think about this question as you read. You will have the answer by the end of the unit.

Dirt

by Steve Tomecek

illustrated by Nancy Woodman

Some people think that dirt is just something to be cleaned up—like the stuff you wash out of your clothes. But dirt is really one of the most important things on earth.

Chapter 6

Looking at Our Earth

natural resource

mineral

boulders

soil

humus

natural resource

A natural resource is something from Earth that people use.

mineral

A mineral is a nonliving thing found in nature.

soil

Soil is the loose top layer of Earth.

humus

Humus is bits of rotting plants and animals in soil.

What Covers Earth?

Science and You

You need fresh water to live and grow.

Inquiry Skill

Use Numbers You can count things to find out how amounts are alike or different.

STANDARDS
SC.H.1.1.4.1.1. uses simple graphs, pictures, written statements, and numbers to observe, describe, record, and compare data.

What You Need

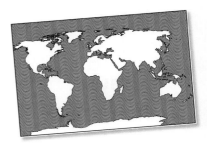

map

counters

paper and marker

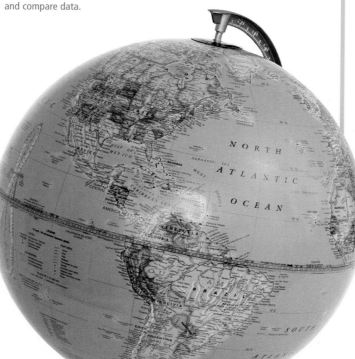

Land and Water

Steps

1. Use green counters to cover all the land on the map. Use blue counters to cover all the water.

2. **Classify** Sort the counters into two groups called **Land** and **Water**.

3. **Use Numbers** Count each group of counters. Record your data.

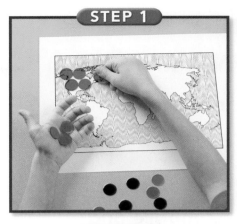
STEP 1

STEP 2

STEP 3

Think and Share

1. **Use Data** Did more counters cover land or water?

2. **Infer** Why do you think Earth is called the water planet?

Investigate More!

Work Together Work with your classmates. Find or draw pictures of things that live on land, in water, or in the air. Explain what your pictures show.

▶ **Vocabulary**

natural resource

▶ **Reading Skill**

Compare and Contrast

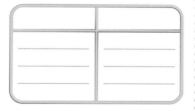

STANDARDS
SC.D.1.1.1.1.1. extends and refines knowledge that the surface of the Earth is composed of different types of solid materials.

Water Resources

A **natural resource** is something from Earth that people use. Air and land are both natural resources. Water is a natural resource, too. Water covers most of Earth.

People use water in many ways. They swim and play in it. They travel on it. They wash and clean with it.

river

ocean

Ocean water is salty. Fresh water is not salty. Fresh water is found in streams, rivers, lakes, and the ground. People need fresh water to drink.

▶ **COMPARE AND CONTRAST** How is lake water different from ocean water?

stream

river

lake

Land and Air Resources

Earth's land and air are natural resources. People use soil to grow plants. They use trees to make paper, furniture, and buildings.

People use rocks to make statues and buildings. They melt sand to make glass.

cotton

oats

tree

sand

Air is a natural resource that living things need. You cannot see air, but you use it every time you breathe.

▶ **COMPARE AND CONTRAST** **How do people use land and air resources?**

Lesson Wrap-Up

❶ **Vocabulary** What do you call something from Earth that people use?

❷ **Reading Skill** How are water and land resources alike? How are they different?

❸ **Use Numbers** What are four objects that are made from plants?

Technology Visit **www.eduplace.com/scp/** to find out more about natural resources.

How Do People Use Rocks and Minerals?

Science and You

People use rocks to make statues and buildings.

Inquiry Skill

Experiment Make a plan to collect data and then communicate the results.

STANDARDS
SC.H.1.1.5.1.1. uses a variety of tools (for example, thermometers, magnifiers, rulers, scales, computers) to identify characteristics of objects.

What You Need

rocks

hand lens

sorting mat

Compare Rocks

Steps

1. **Observe** Use a hand lens to look at each rock. Touch each rock.

STEP 1

2. **Compare** Look for ways in which the rocks are alike. Look for ways in which the rocks are different.

STEP 2

3. **Classify** Sort the rocks into groups. Tell how the rocks in a group are alike.

STEP 3

Think and Share

1. **Communicate** Tell what you learned about the rocks you observed.

2. What are some other ways to sort the rocks?

Investigate More!

Experiment Rub each rock on different materials, such as the back of a tile. Talk with others about what you observe.

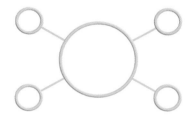
Rocks and Minerals

A **mineral** is a nonliving thing found in nature. A rock is a nonliving thing made of one or more minerals. Rocks and minerals are natural resources.

Different rocks have different minerals in them. That is why they are different colors.

Minerals

▼ **amethyst in a geode**

▼ **cinnabar**

gypsum ▶

Rocks come in many sizes. Some mountains are made of rock. Very large rocks are sometimes called **boulders**. Sand is made of very small rocks or minerals.

▲ sandstone

▶ **MAIN IDEA** What are rocks made of?

Rocks

limestone ▶

granite ▲

◀ obsidian

◀ A conglomerate is made of bits of different rocks.

Using Rocks and Minerals

People use rocks and minerals in different ways. Talc, graphite, and gold are some of the softest minerals. People use them for powder, pencils, and medals. Garnet is harder than graphite. People use garnets for jewelry.

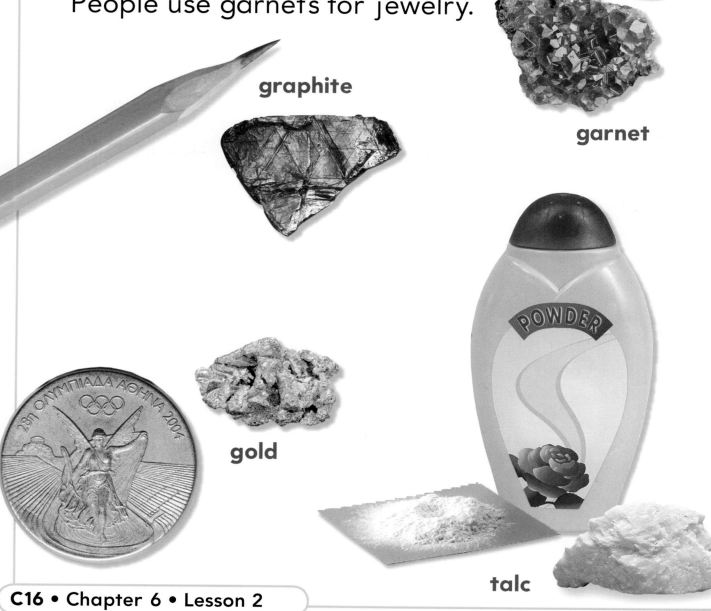

graphite

garnet

gold

POWDER

talc

People use hard rocks for buildings, statues, and bridges. Limestone, sandstone, and granite are hard rocks.

▶ **MAIN IDEA** What are some ways that people use rocks and minerals?

limestone

▲ **Chicago Water Tower**

Lesson Wrap-Up

❶ **Vocabulary** What is a **mineral**?

❷ **Reading Skill** Tell three things you know about rocks and minerals.

❸ **Experiment** How can experimenting with rocks help you learn about them?

Technology Visit **www.eduplace.com/scp/** to find out more about rocks and minerals.

Rock Stars

Cast
Narrator
Paul: a sculptor
Susan: a jeweler
Art: a builder
Jon: a road worker
Carla: a miner

STANDARDS
SC.D.1.1.1.1.1. extends and refines knowledge that the surface of the Earth is composed of different types of solid materials.

READING LINK

Narrator: People use rocks in many ways. Some jobs depend on rocks.

Paul: I am a sculptor. I carve rocks to make art.

Carla: What kind of rocks do you use?

Paul: I use marble. Marble is a pretty rock. It is very strong, too.

Art: I am a builder. I use rocks that are hard and pretty, too! I like sandstone and granite.

Susan: What do you use them for?

Art: I cut and polish rocks to make blocks and tiles. I use the blocks and tiles in buildings.

Susan: I am a jeweler. I cut and polish pretty rocks, too. I use them to make jewelry.

Jon: I am a road worker. I use crushed rocks, like limestone, to make concrete to build roads.

Carla: Very interesting. But you would not have jobs without me!

Paul, Susan, Art, and Jon: Why?

Carla: I am a miner. I dig up rocks from the ground. Then people like you can use them!

Paul, Susan, Art, and Jon: Thanks Carla! You rock!

Sharing Ideas

1. **Write About It** Glass is made from melted sand. Write a story telling how a glassmaker is a rock star.
2. **Talk About It** What would your life be like without rocks?

What Is Soil?

Science and You

You may think that soil is just dirt, but it is an important natural resource.

Inquiry Skill

Observe Use your senses to learn about soil.

goggles

soil

toothpick

hand lens

STANDARDS
SC.H.1.1.5.1.1. uses a variety of tools (for example, thermometers, magnifiers, rulers, scales, computers) to identify characteristics of objects.

Observe Soil

Steps

STEP 1

1 **Observe** Spread apart the bits of soil. Look at the soil with a hand lens. Record what you see. **Safety:** Wear goggles!

2 Squeeze a handful of soil. Slowly open your hand. Record what happens.

STEP 2

3 Rub some soil between your hands. Tell how the soil feels. **Safety:** Wash your hands!

STEP 3

Think and Share

1. What do you think soil is made of?

2. **Infer** Why do you think the soil stuck together?

Investigate More!

Experiment Find out about other kinds of soil. With an adult, dig soil from two different places. Compare the small parts in each kind of soil.

Soil

Soil is the loose top layer of Earth. Soil is made of bits of minerals and rock, rotting plants, and rotting animals. The bits of rotting plants and animals are called **humus**. The rocks, minerals, and humus help plants grow. Some water and air are also found in soil.

Kinds of Soil

Topsoil	Clay Soil	Sandy Soil
• black or brown • best for plant growth	• brown, red, or yellow • sticky when wet	• tan or light brown • holds little water

Soil is a natural resource. Most plants need soil to grow. Many animals live in soil. They help the soil by digging in it and breaking it into small pieces. This keeps air in the soil. It makes space for water to get into the soil, too.

▶ **CAUSE AND EFFECT** How do animals help soil?

earthworm

wood lice

Saving Soil

It is important to save soil because it takes a long time for soil to form. Water and wind can take soil away. One way to save soil is to grow plants. The plant roots help hold soil in place.

soil with plants

soil without plants

Lesson Wrap-Up

❶ **Vocabulary** What is **soil**?

❷ **Reading Skill** What causes soil to go away?

❸ **Observe** What can you learn about soil by observing it?

Technology Visit **www.eduplace.com/scp/** to find out more about soil.

LINKS
for Home and School

Math **Make a Pictograph**

Take a class survey. Count the number of children whose families grow flowers, vegetables, or houseplants. Record your data in a pictograph.

How We Use Soil	
To Grow Flowers	☺☺☺☺☺☺☺☺☺☺
To Grow Vegetables	☺☺☺☺☺☺
To Grow Houseplants	☺☺☺☺

Each ☺ stands for 1 child.

Music **This Land Is Your Land**

Sing "This Land Is Your Land." Then draw a picture to show how people use the land where you live.

Visual Summary

Earth has many natural resources.

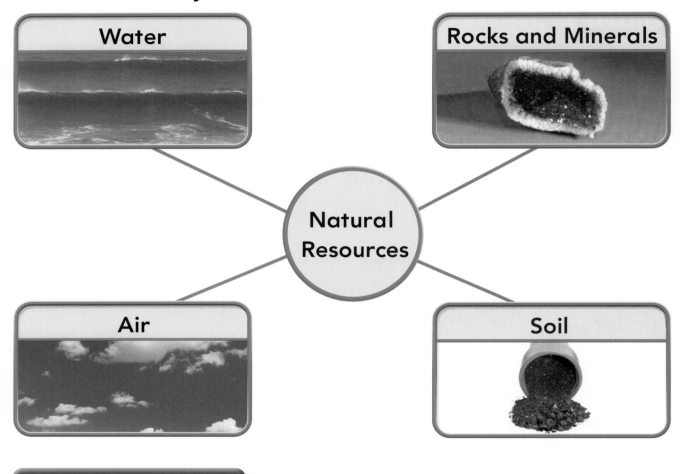

Water

Rocks and Minerals

Natural Resources

Air

Soil

Main Ideas

1. Why is water a natural resource? (pp. C8–C9)

2. Name three resources from land. (pp. C10–C11)

3. What are two things that people use rocks and minerals for? (pp. C16–C17)

4. What is soil made of? (p. C24)

Vocabulary and Science Skills

Choose the correct answer.

5. Bits of rotting plants and animals in soil are called _____.

○ rock   ○ humus   ○ minerals

6. Which is a natural resource?

○ glass   ○ air   ○ sandwich

7. Which is made of very small rocks?

○ sand   ○ mountains   ○ boulders

8. Rocks are made of one or more _____.

○ mountains   ○ animals   ○ minerals

9. Which can help save soil?

○ plants   ○ water   ○ wind

10. Which is made from trees?

○ paper   ○ crayon   ○ chalk

Chapter 7

Caring for Our Earth

air pollution

water
  pollution

reuse

recycle

reduce

air pollution

Air pollution happens when harmful things get into air.

water pollution

Water pollution happens when harmful things get into water.

reuse

Reuse means to use something again.

recycle

When you recycle an object, a factory takes it and makes a new object from it.

How Do We Use Air?

Science and You

You use air every time you breathe.

Inquiry Skill

Use Data You can use what you observe and record to learn more about something.

STANDARDS
SC.H.1.1.2.1.1. understands the importance of accuracy and repetition in conducting scientific inquiries.

What You Need

petroleum jelly

2 index cards

hand lens

Collect Pollution

Steps

1. Spread petroleum jelly on two index cards.

2. Place one card outdoors. Place the other card indoors.

3. **Observe** Wait three days. Then use a hand lens to look at the cards.

4. **Record Data** Draw or write what you see.

STEP 1

STEP 2

STEP 3

Think and Share

1. **Infer** Where did the dust and dirt come from?

2. **Use Data** Compare the two cards. Which card has more dust and dirt? Tell why.

Investigate More!

Experiment Repeat the experiment two more times. Predict what will happen. Then tell why you think the results were the same or different each time.

▶ **Vocabulary**

air pollution

▶ **Reading Skill**

Draw Conclusions

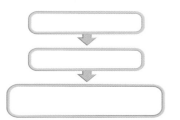

STANDARDS
SC.G.2.1.2.1.1. understands that there are limited resources available for all living things to use.

Air

Air is a natural resource. People, plants, and animals need air to stay alive. You cannot see air, but you can feel it push against you. Sometimes you can smell things in the air.

▼ **The boy blows air into the bubbles.**

People use air in many ways. A sailboat uses air to move across the water. You can use air to cool off on a hot day. Moving air can help make electricity to run things like TVs and lamps.

▶ **DRAW CONCLUSIONS** Why is air important?

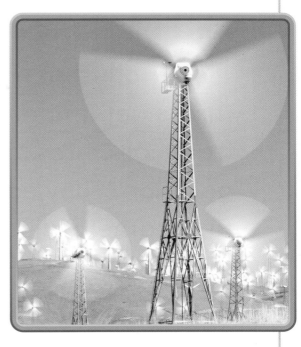

▲ **Windmills help make electricity.**

Air pushes on the sail.

Air Pollution

Air pollution happens when harmful things get into air. Dust and smoke from cars, fires, and factories are pollution. They can make air harmful to breathe. Pollution can make living things sick.

air pollution

clean air

Clean air helps plants grow and stay green. It helps animals and people have healthy lungs. Clean air also keeps buildings and statues clean.

▶ **DRAW CONCLUSIONS**
Why is it important to keep air clean?

Pollution is being cleaned off.

Lesson Wrap-Up

❶ **Vocabulary** What causes **air pollution**?

❷ **Reading Skill** Why does a fire cause air pollution?

❸ **Use Data** If you find bits of dirt on a windowsill, what do you know about the air?

🖳 **Technology** Visit **www.eduplace.com/scp/** to find out more about air.

How Do We Use Water?

Science and You

When you ride in a boat you are using water.

Inquiry Skill

Use Models Use something like a real thing to learn how the real thing works.

STANDARDS
SC.H.1.1.3.1.1. works with others to complete an experiment or to solve a problem.

What You Need

wire

self-stick notes

spool

water

tub

A Waterwheel

Steps

1. Put self-stick notes on the edges of a spool.

STEP 1

2. Put wire through the spool to make a waterwheel. **Safety:** Use wire carefully!

STEP 2

3. **Use Models** Hold the waterwheel over a tub. Slowly pour water over a side of the waterwheel. Record what happens.

STEP 3

Think and Share

1. **Communicate** Tell what happened to the spool.

2. **Infer** What made the spool turn?

Investigate More!

Experiment Make a waterwheel that turns faster. Use objects such as clay, cardboard, and tape. Share your results.

Vocabulary
water pollution

Reading Skill
Categorize and Classify

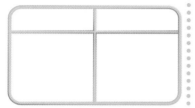

STANDARDS
SC.D.2.1.1.1.1. extends and refines knowledge of ways to care for the Earth at home and in school.
SC.G.2.1.2.1.1. understands that there are limited resources available for all living things to use.

Water

Water is found in lakes, rivers, oceans, and under the ground. Water is a natural resource that you cannot live without.

You use water every day. You drink water. You use water when you take a bath. You use it when you swim, cook, clean, and water plants.

drinking ▶

◀ washing

People use water to put out fires. They use water in lakes, rivers, and oceans when they fish, swim, or travel. People also use moving water to make electricity.

▶ **CLASSIFY** What are three ways people use water?

▲ having fun

▲ fighting fires

▲ Water in a dam is used to make electricity.

Water Pollution

Water pollution happens when harmful things get into water. Putting trash and oil in water causes water pollution. Polluted water can kill plants. It can make animals and people sick if they drink or swim in it.

cleaning an oil-covered bird

oil slick

People can help clean up pollution. They can pick up trash. They can clean up oil. They can stop putting harmful things into the water, too!

▶ **CLASSIFY How can people clean up water pollution?**

Lesson Wrap-Up

1. **Vocabulary** What happens when harmful things get into water?

2. **Reading Skill** What are two things that cause water pollution?

3. **Use Models** How can using a model help you learn about water and its uses?

Technology Visit **www.eduplace.com/scp/** to find out more about water.

Safety at the Beach

Florida has a lot of beaches where you can swim. Having a good time means having a safe time. Here are some ways to stay safe at the beach.

BEACH WARNING FLAGS
BANDERAS DE ADVERTENSIA EN LA PLAYA

Water Closed to Public
Agua Cerrada al Publico

High Hazard
High Surf and/or Strong Currents
Peligro Alto. Resaca Alta y/o Corrientes Fuertes

Medium Hazard
Moderate Surf and/or Currents
Peligro Medio. Resaca Moderada y/o Corrientes Fuertes

Low Hazard
Calm Conditions, Exercise Caution
Peligro Bajo. Condiciones Calmas. Tenga cuidado

Dangerous Marine Life
Vida Marina Peligrosa

Absence of Flags Does Not Assure Safe Waters
La ausencia de Banderas No Asegura Aguas Seguras

Colored flags let you know if it is safe to swim.

Swimming Safety

1. Always swim where there is a lifeguard.

2. Be sure an adult is watching you.

3. Stay out of the water in stormy weather.

4. Only swim when the water is calm.

5. Stay away from jellyfish. They can sting you.

Sharing Ideas

1. **Write About It** Write about how you can stay safe at the beach.

2. **Talk About It** Why is it important to listen to lifeguards?

How Can We Help Earth?

Science and You

You can help Earth by recycling cans, bottles, and paper.

Inquiry Skill

Classify Group things that are alike in some way.

What You Need

trash objects

index cards

marker

STANDARDS
SC.H.1.1.3.1.1. works with others to complete an experiment or to solve a problem.

Sort Your Trash

Steps

1. **Classify** Think about what each object is made of. Sort objects into groups.

STEP 1

2. **Record Data** Put an index card next to each group. Write a name for the group on each card.

STEP 2

3. Write on each card three ways you could reuse objects in that group.

STEP 3

Think and Share

1. **Compare** How are the objects in each group alike?

2. **Infer** Why might it be a good idea to use some trash again?

Investigate More!

Solve a Problem How much paper does your class throw away in one week? Collect the paper in a trash bag. Then think of ways to save paper.

▶ Vocabulary

reuse

recycle

reduce

▶ Reading Skill

Sequence

STANDARDS
SC.D.2.1.1.1.1. extends and refines knowledge of ways to care for the Earth at home and in school.
SC.G.2.1.2.1.1. understands that there are limited resources available for all living things to use.

▲ **pencil holder**

Reuse

Earth's natural resources may not last forever. You can save resources if you reuse, recycle, and reduce trash.

When you **reuse**, you use something again. This means that resources are not used to make a new thing.

▼ **tire swing and tire sandals**

Watts Towers reuse tiles, metal, and glass. ▶

Think about how you can reuse something before you throw it away. Use a milk carton to plant flowers. Use pictures in old magazines to make cards. Reusing can help natural resources last longer.

▶ **SEQUENCE** What should you think about before you throw something away?

▲ **license-plate purse**

Recycle

When you **recycle** an object, a factory takes it and makes a new object from it. People recycle newspapers, paper, plastic, and cans. They also recycle glass, rubber, batteries, and cardboard.

plastic bottles

backpack

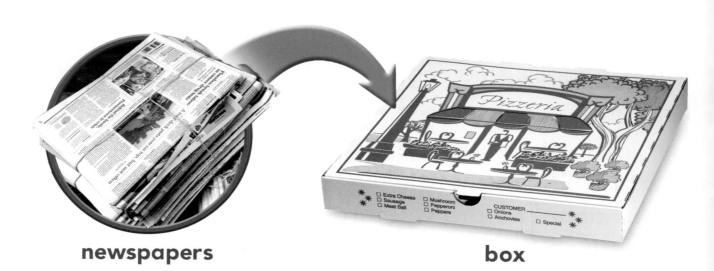

newspapers

box

First, things go to recycling centers. Second, factories make the recycled things into resources again. Third, the resources are made into new things that you can use.

▶ **SEQUENCE** What happens when things are recycled?

old cans

new cans

old sneaker

running track

Reduce

When you **reduce**, you use less of something. Try to use up old crayons before you get new ones. Take care of your things so that they last longer.

The picture shows other ways you can reduce what you use.

• Turn off water while you brush your teeth.

• Use paper and plastic bags more than one time.

• Write or draw on both sides of paper.

Lesson Wrap-Up

❶ **Vocabulary** What does it mean to **recycle**?

❷ **Reading Skill** List the steps in recycling.

❸ **Classify** Do you reuse, recycle, or reduce when you use an old can as a trash can?

 Technology Visit **www.eduplace.com/scp/** to find out more about recycling.

Math Sort and Count Plastic

Collect and wash all the plastic bottles you use in five days. Look for a number on the bottom of each bottle. Make a chart to record what you find.

Kinds of Plastic Bottles	
Kind	Number
Number 1	7
Number 2	4
Number 3	1

Write a number sentence to show how many number 1 and number 2 bottles you have.

Social Studies Keep It Clean

Everyone can help keep air, land, and water clean. Make a poster to remind people to clean up after themselves.

Visual Summary

There are many ways to care for Earth.

Keep air, water, and land clean	Reuse	Recycle	Reduce
			• Turn off water while you brush your teeth. • Use paper and plastic bags more than one time. • Write or draw on both sides of paper.

Main Ideas

1. What are two ways that people use air? **(pp. C34–C35)**

2. What are three ways that people use water? **(pp. C40–C41)**

3. Why is water pollution harmful? **(p. C42)**

4. What happens when you reduce? **(p. C52)**

Vocabulary and Science Skills

Choose the correct answer.

5. Using an old tire as a swing is _____.

○ reducing   ○ recycling   ○ reusing

6. Which can cause air pollution?

○ smoke   ○ trash   ○ trees

7. Which means to use less of something?

○ reduce   ○ recycle   ○ reuse

8. Which can cause water pollution?

○ birds   ○ oil   ○ plants

9. Which do you save when you use both sides of paper?

○ natural resource   ○ can   ○ bottle

10. People use air when they _____.

○ breathe   ○ cook   ○ drink

Discover!

Why do rocks have different colors?

Rocks are made of one or more minerals. Minerals are different colors because of the way they are formed. The color of a rock depends on the minerals inside the rock.

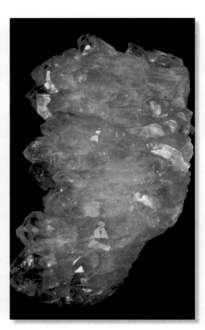

Go to **www.eduplace.com/scp/** to see rocks and their colors.

EARTH SCIENCE

UNIT D

Weather and the Sky

Cricket Connection

Visit www.eduplace.com/scp/ to check out *Click, Ask,* and *Odyssey* magazine articles and activities.

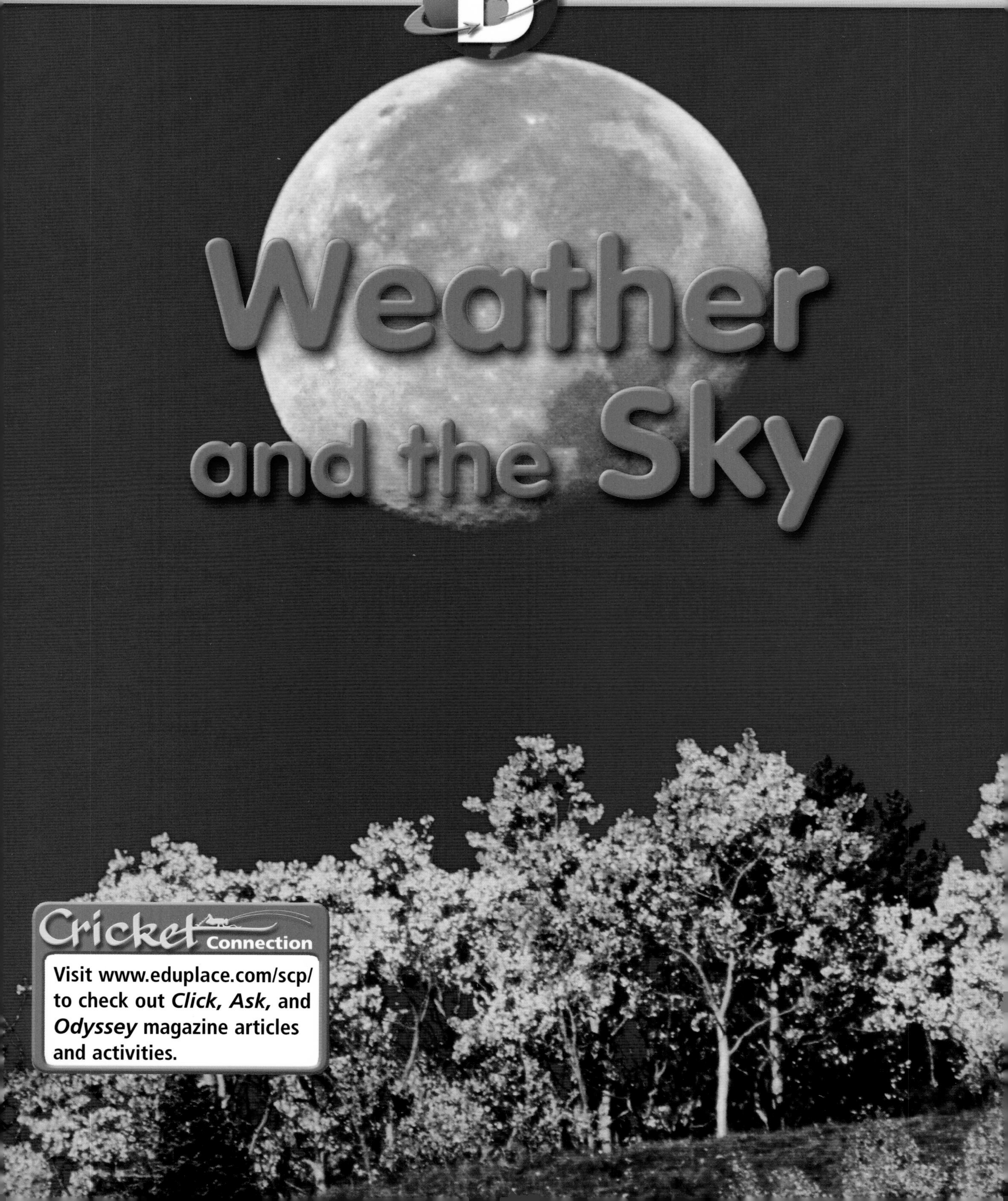

Florida Weather

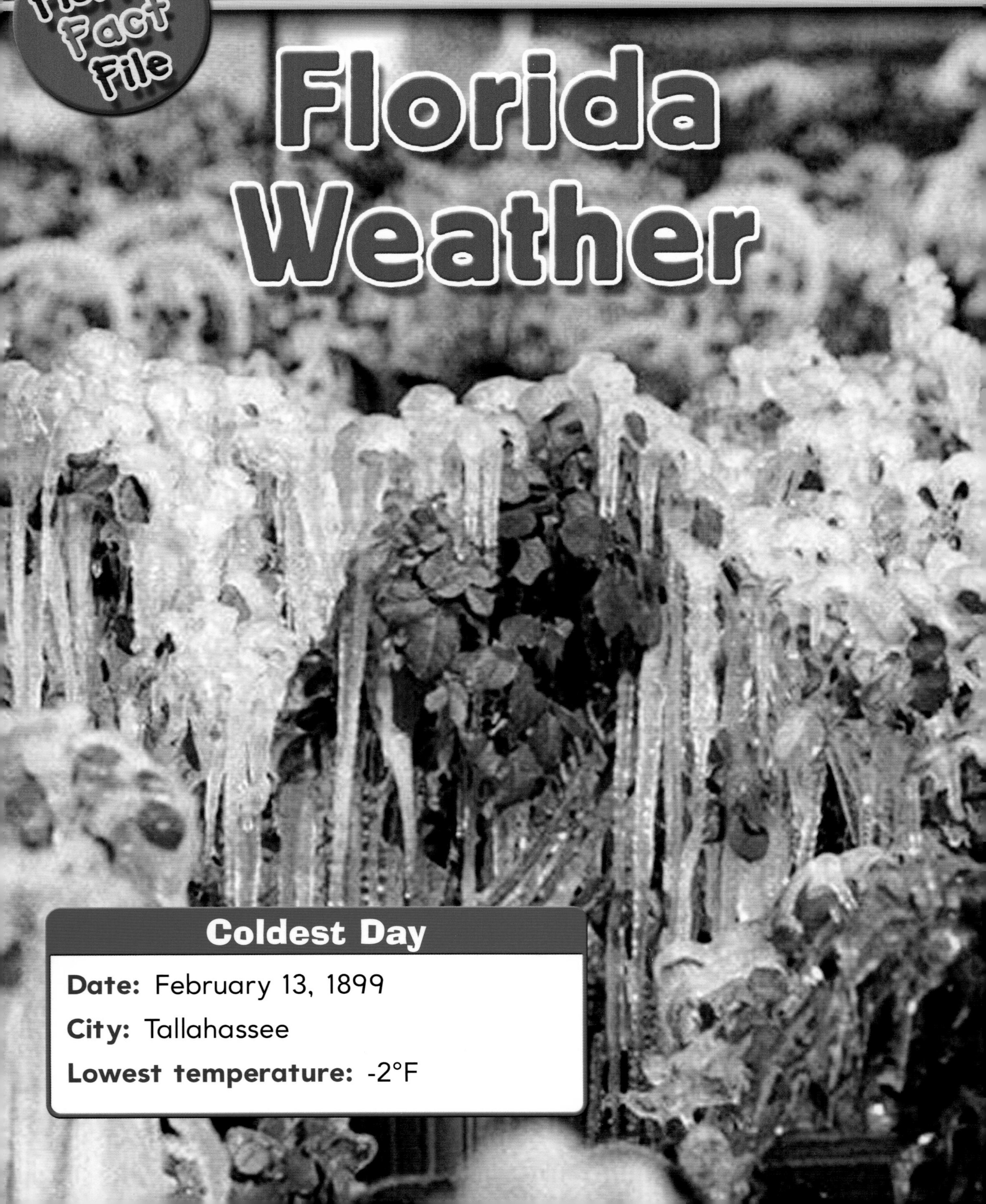

Coldest Day

Date: February 13, 1899

City: Tallahassee

Lowest temperature: -2°F

Most Snow in One Day

Date: March 6, 1954

City: Milton

Snowfall: 4 inches

Most Rain in One Day

Date: September 5, 1950

City: Yankeetown

Rainfall: 38.7 inches

ROAD UNDER WATER

Hottest Day

Date: June 29, 1931

City: Monticello

Highest temperature: 109°F

Weather
and the Sky

Reading in Science.............**D2**

Chapter 8
Weather and Seasons **D4**

Chapter 9
Changes in the Sky **D42**

Independent Reading

Time to Sleep

Measuring Weather

Clouds

Discover!

Where are the stars during the day?

Think about this question as you read. You will have the answer by the end of the unit.

What Will the Weather Be?

by Lynda DeWitt

illustrated by Carolyn Croll

Weather forecasts tell us what kind of weather is coming. But predicting the weather is hard to do. It is easy to see what the weather is like right now. You can go outside and look.

Chapter 8

Weather and Seasons

weather

thermometer

temperature

water cycle

cloud

season

spring

summer

fall

winter

weather

Weather is what the air outside is like.

thermometer

A thermometer is a tool that measures temperature.

cloud

Many drops of water together form a cloud.

season

A season is a time of year that has its own kind of weather.

What Is Weather?

Science and You

Observing the weather can help you decide to play inside or outside.

Inquiry Skill

Record Data You can use pictures to show what you observe.

STANDARDS
SC.H.1.1.4.1.1. uses simple graphs, pictures, written statements, and numbers to observe, describe, record, and compare data.

What You Need

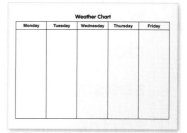

weather chart

weather pictures

scissors

glue

Record Weather

Steps

1. **Observe** Look outside to see the weather today.

STEP 1

2. Cut out pictures that show the weather today. **Safety:** Scissors are sharp!

STEP 2

3. **Record Data** Glue the pictures in your weather chart.

4. Repeat each day for one week.

STEP 3

Think and Share

1. What does your chart tell you about the weather?

2. Why might you record two pictures for the same day?

Investigate More!

Work Together Record the weather for two more weeks. Talk with others. Were their data the same or different? Tell why.

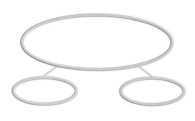

Learn by Reading

► **Vocabulary**

weather

► **Reading Skill**

Main Idea and Details

STANDARDS
SC.D.1.1.3.1.1. uses graphic organizers to display weather data and show weather patterns.

Kinds of Weather

Weather is what the air outside is like. There are many kinds of weather. Weather may be warm or cool. It may be rainy or sunny. It may be cloudy or windy.

How do you know it is warm and sunny here?

You can use your senses to observe the weather. You can see clouds. You can hear rain. You can feel warm or cool air. You can see wind move things.

▶ **MAIN IDEA** What are some kinds of weather?

rainy ▼

▲ windy and cloudy

Ways Weather Changes

Monday	cloudy	
Tuesday	rainy 	
Wednesday	sunny 	

Weather Changes

Weather changes when the air changes. <u>Weather can change from day to day.</u> One day the weather can be sunny and warm. The next day it can be cloudy and cool. Then clouds may bring rain.

▶ **MAIN IDEA** How might weather change from day to day?

Lesson Wrap-Up

❶ **Vocabulary** Tell something that you know about **weather**.

❷ **Reading Skill** How can you use your senses to observe weather?

❸ **Record Data** Tell one way to record data.

🖥 **Technology** Visit **www.eduplace.com/scp/** to find out more about weather.

How Can You Measure Weather?

Science and You

Reading a thermometer helps you know when you might need a jacket.

Inquiry Skill

Measure Use a tool to find how much or how many.

STANDARDS
SC.H.1.1.5.1.1. uses a variety of tools (for example, thermometers, magnifiers, rulers, scales, computers) to identify characteristics of objects.

What You Need

measuring chart

thermometer

ruler

rain collector

Measure Weather

Steps

1. Take the thermometer and the rain collector outside.

STEP 1

2. **Record Data** Go outside again later. Read the thermometer. Record the temperature.

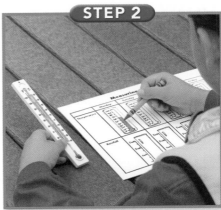

STEP 2

3. **Measure** Use a ruler to measure any rain. Record what you measure. Empty the rain collector.

4. Do these steps for five days.

STEP 3

Think and Share

1. How did tools help you learn about weather?

2. How did the weather change during the five days?

Investigate More!

Be an Inventor Invent a tool to show if wind is blowing. Try your tool. Explain how your tool works.

▶ **Vocabulary**

thermometer
temperature

▶ **Reading Skill**
Draw
Conclusions

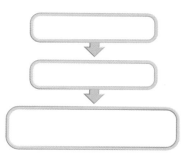

STANDARDS
SC.H.3.1.1.1.1. knows that scientists and technologists use a variety of tools (e.g., thermometers, magnifiers, rulers, and scales) to obtain information in more detail and make work easier.

A Tool for Temperature

One way to tell about weather is to use tools. A **thermometer** is a tool that measures temperature. **Temperature** is how warm or cool something is.

What do these thermometers tell about the weather?

Knowing the temperature helps you know what to wear. When the temperature is cold, you wear clothes that keep you warm. When it is hot, you wear clothes that keep you cool.

▶ **DRAW CONCLUSIONS If you need a coat, what can you tell about the temperature?**

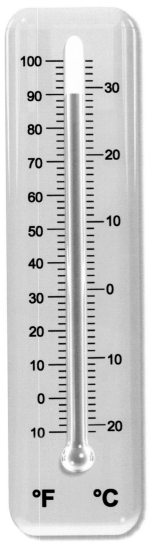

Tools for Wind and Rain

You can use tools to measure wind and rain. A windsock and a wind vane show which way the wind blows. A windsock also shows how hard the wind blows. A rain gauge measures how much rain falls.

▶ **DRAW CONCLUSIONS** If a rain gauge is full, what can you tell about the weather?

▼ **windsock**

wind vane ▼

rain gauge ▶

Lesson Wrap-Up

❶ **Vocabulary** What is **temperature**?

❷ **Reading Skill** If a windsock is hanging down, what can you tell about the wind?

❸ **Measure** How can you describe weather?

🖥 **Technology** Visit **www.eduplace.com/scp/** to find out more about weather tools.

Read the page from the story. Then read the poem. Compare how the writers observe rain.

Rain

by Manya Stojic

A raindrop splashed.
"The rain is here!"
said the rhino.

"Porcupine smelled it.
The zebras saw it.
The baboons heard it.
And I felt it.
I must tell the lion."

City Rain

by Rachel Field

Rain in the city!
  I love to see it fall
Slantwise where the
buildings crowd
  Red brick and all,
Streets of shiny wetness
  Where the taxis go,
With people and umbrellas all
  Bobbing to and fro.

Sharing Ideas

1. **Write About It** How do the animals and the poet know it is raining?

2. **Talk About It** What is one thing in the story that real animals cannot do?

What Are Clouds and Rain?

Science and You

If you see dark clouds in the sky, you know it might rain.

Inquiry Skill

Compare Look for ways that objects are alike and different.

STANDARDS
SC.H.2.1.1.1.1. uses information gathered to identify patterns in nature to make predictions (for example, shapes of leaves, petals on flowers, rings on seashells).

What You Need

2 cups

water

tape

plastic wrap

grease pencil

Water Changes

Steps

1. **Measure** Put the same amount of water into each cup. Cover one cup.

2. Mark the water level on each cup.

3. **Predict** Put the cups in a sunny place. Tell how the water might change.

4. **Observe** Look at the cups every day for a week. Record what you see.

STEP 1

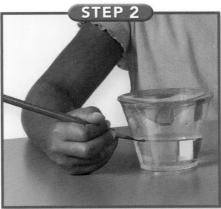
STEP 2

STEP 3

Think and Share

1. **Compare** How did the water change in each cup?

2. **Infer** Why do you think the water changed?

Investigate More!

Ask Questions What else can you do to make water change? Finish the question. What would happen to the water if I _____?

▶ **Vocabulary** FCAT

water cycle
cloud

▶ **Reading Skill**
Cause and
Effect

STANDARDS
SC.B.1.1.3.1.1. understands that
models (for example, terrarium or
aquarium) can be used to observe
processes and changes over time.

Water Cycle

Water moves from place to place. Sometimes it seems to disappear. Water moving from Earth to the sky and back again is called the **water cycle**.

▶ **CAUSE AND EFFECT**
What causes water to go into the air?

1
Heat from the Sun warms water. Some warm water goes into the air. You cannot see this water.

2 Water in the air cools. Tiny drops of water form. Many drops of water together form a **cloud**.

3 Water drops in the clouds get bigger. Then they fall back to Earth as rain or sleet.

Kinds of Clouds

There are many kinds of clouds. They have different shapes and colors. Looking at clouds gives you clues about changing weather.

▶ **CAUSE AND EFFECT** What can clouds tell you about changing weather?

Cirrus clouds are thin and feathery. They mean it may rain in a day or two.

Cumulus clouds are puffy and white. They can turn gray and bring rain.

Stratus clouds are low and gray. They may bring rain or snow.

Lesson Wrap-Up

❶ **Vocabulary** What is the **water cycle**?

❷ **Reading Skill** What causes rain to fall?

❸ **Compare** Draw two kinds of clouds. Tell how they are alike and different.

Technology Visit **www.eduplace.com/scp/** to find out more about clouds.

What Is Weather Like in Spring and Summer?

Science and You

Spring is a time when you may see flowers bloom.

Inquiry Skill

Communicate Tell other people what you know by drawing, speaking, or writing.

STANDARDS
SC.H.1.1.3.1.1. works with others to complete an experiment or to solve a problem.

What You Need

2 cups

paper towels

seeds

water

Grow Plants

Steps

1. Spray water on the paper towels. Fill each cup with paper towels.

2. Add seeds to each cup.

3. **Predict** Put the **winter** cup in a cold place. Put the **spring** cup in a warm place. Tell what you think will happen.

4. **Communicate** Look at the seeds after five days. Talk about how they have changed.

STEP 1

STEP 2

STEP 3

Think and Share

1. What helped the seeds grow?

2. **Infer** What happens to seeds in cold weather?

Investigate More!

Experiment Put the sprouted seeds in soil. Make a plan for caring for the plants. Follow your plan. Observe the plants for one month.

▶ **Vocabulary**

season

spring

summer

▶ **Reading Skill**
Compare and Contrast

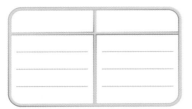

STANDARDS
SC.F.2.1.2.1.3. knows some ways in which animals and plants are adapted to living in different environments.
SC.G.1.1.2.1.1. knows that plants produce oxygen and food for animals.

Spring

A **season** is a time of year that has its own kind of weather. **Spring** is the season that follows winter. There are more hours of daylight in spring than in winter.

In spring, the weather begins to get warmer. Warmer weather and spring rain help plants grow.

Spring plants begin to grow.

The warm weather and new plants make it easy for animals to find food. Animals that slept all winter are now awake. Birds that flew to other places in winter have come back. Many baby animals are born in spring.

goose with gosling

▶ **COMPARE AND CONTRAST**
How is spring different from winter?

Luna Moth in Spring

1. A caterpillar eats a leaf.

2. A caterpillar spins a cocoon.

3. A caterpillar changes to a moth.

Summer

Summer is the season that follows spring. Summer is the warmest season of the year. It has the most hours of daylight.

In summer, people try to find ways to stay cool. They wear clothing that keeps them cool. They might go swimming to cool off.

peach tree

How is this girl keeping cool?

Summer is the season for plants and animals to grow. Plants grow in the warm summer sun. Fruits form on trees and bushes. Young animals grow in summer, too. They learn to find their own food.

Growing plants are food for the lamb.

 **COMPARE AND CONTRAST**
How are spring and summer different?

Lesson Wrap-Up

❶ Vocabulary What is a **season**?

❷ Reading Skill How are spring and summer alike?

❸ Communicate Write a story or draw a picture. Tell what happens to plants or animals in spring or summer.

Technology Visit **www.eduplace.com/scp/** to find out more about seasons.

What Is Weather Like in Fall and Winter?

Science and You

When you know about the seasons, you know what kind of weather is coming next.

Inquiry Skill

Classify Group objects that are alike in some way.

 STANDARDS
SC.H.1.1.3.1.1. works with others to complete an experiment or to solve a problem.

spinner

paper squares

crayons

paper

What to Wear

Steps

1. Take turns spinning the spinner.

2. **Communicate** Name a clothing item you might wear in that season. Draw the item you name.

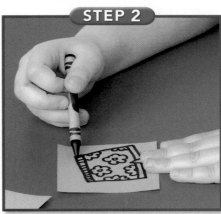

3. **Classify** Sort the clothing pictures by season. Label each group.

Think and Share

1. **Compare** How are all the summer clothes you drew alike?

2. What clothes keep you warm in cool weather?

Investigate More!

Solve a Problem Suppose your cousins are coming to visit you in winter. What kind of clothes would you tell them to bring?

► **Vocabulary**

fall

winter

► **Reading Skill**

Sequence

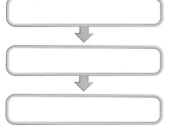

STANDARDS
SC.F.2.1.2.1.2. knows the
characteristics of the climate
in different habitats.
SC.D.1.1.3.1.1. uses
graphic organizers to display
weather data and show
weather patterns.

Fall

Fall is the season that follows summer. There are fewer hours of daylight in fall than in summer.

In fall, the weather gets cooler. People wear warmer clothes. Some leaves turn color and fall to the ground. Many fruits and vegetables are ripe.

Geese fly to warm places in fall.

In fall, animals get ready for cold weather. Some animals grow thicker fur to keep warm. Many animals store food for winter. Other animals move to places where there is more food. They will return in spring.

▶ **SEQUENCE** What season comes before winter?

A squirrel stores food for winter.

Winter

Winter is the season that follows fall. Winter has the fewest hours of daylight. It is the coldest season of the year. In some places, snow falls and water freezes. In other places, winter weather is warmer.

winter where weather is warm ▶

◀ winter where weather is cold

▲ **Why is it hard for animals to find food here?**

Sometimes it is hard for animals to find food in winter. Some plants die. Many trees lose their leaves. Many animals eat food that they gathered in fall. Some animals sleep all winter.

▶ **SEQUENCE** What season follows winter?

The Pattern of Seasons

The seasons change in the same order every year. Living things change with the seasons.

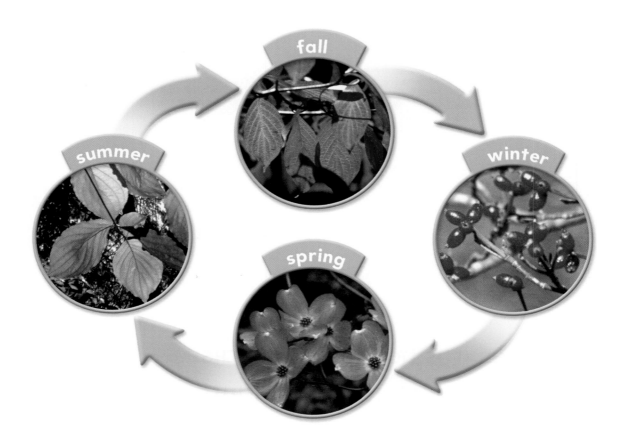

Lesson Wrap-Up

❶ **Vocabulary** What is **winter**?

❷ **Reading Skill** What season comes before fall?

❸ **Classify** Name three signs of fall.

Technology Visit **www.eduplace.com/scp/** to find out more about seasons.

L I N K S
for Home and School

Math Read a Bar Graph

Ms. Lane's class made a bar graph to show the weather for ten days.

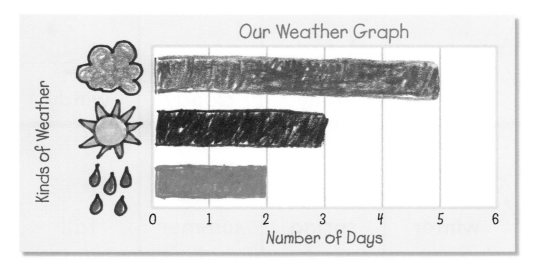

1. How many days were sunny?

2. How many more days were cloudy than rainy?

Social Studies Winter Weather

Winter is cold in many places. But winter is warm or hot in some places. Tell about winter where you live. Draw a picture of yourself in winter.

Winter is warm where I live.

Visual Summary

Weather changes from day to day and from season to season.

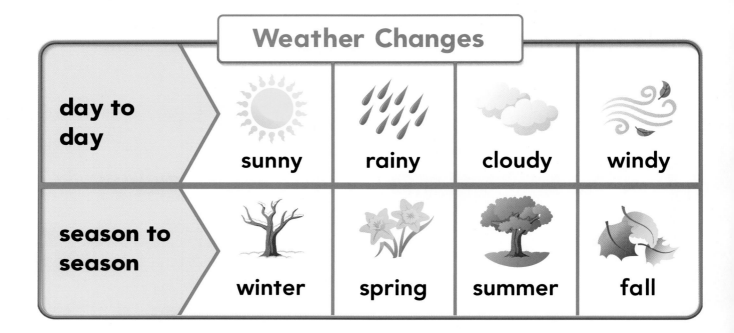

Weather Changes

day to day	sunny	rainy	cloudy	windy
season to season	winter	spring	summer	fall

Main Ideas

1. What are some kinds of weather? **(p. D8)**

2. What can you tell by looking at clouds? **(p. D24)**

3. What is a season? **(p. D28)**

4. How does weather change from summer to fall? **(p. D34)**

Vocabulary and Science Skills

Choose the correct answer.

5. Which tool measures temperature?

○ ruler   ○ thermometer   ○ rain gauge

6. Many drops of water together form a
_____.

○ cloud   ○ season   ○ temperature

7. Which is the coldest season of the year?

○ summer   ○ fall   ○ winter

8. Which is the warmest season of the year?

○ summer   ○ spring   ○ winter

9. Water moving from Earth to sky and back
again is the _____.

○ spring   ○ water cycle   ○ weather

10. What always happens on windy days?

○ The ground is wet.   ○ The sky is sunny.
○ Tree branches move.

Changes in the Sky

Sun

star

planet

rotates

Moon

shadow

Sun

The Sun is the brightest space object in the day sky.

star

A star is a space object that makes its own light.

planet

A planet is a space object that moves around the Sun.

Moon

The Moon is a space object close to Earth.

What Can You See in the Sky?

Science and You

You can tell whether it is day or night by looking at the sky.

Inquiry Skill

Observe Use your senses to find out about something.

 STANDARDS
SC.H.1.1.3.1.2. listens, records, and compares the ideas and observations of others.

What You Need

paper and pencil

drawing paper

crayons

Observe the Sky

Steps

STEP 1

1. **Observe** Go outdoors and look at the sky. Make a list of what you see. **Safety:** Do not look right at the Sun!

STEP 2

2. **Record Data** Go inside. Use your list. Draw a picture of what you saw.

3. **Compare** Ask others what they observed. Compare your drawings.

STEP 3

Think and Share

1. What did you and your classmates see in the day sky?

2. Did anything surprise you? Tell why.

Investigate More!

Work Together Observe the night sky. Draw what you see. Ask others what they saw. Tell how the night sky is different from the day sky.

Vocabulary FCAT

Sun

star

planet

Reading Skill

Compare and Contrast

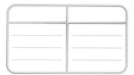

STANDARDS
SC.E.2.1.1.1.1. knows and differentiates objects seen in the day and night sky (for example, clouds, Sun, stars, Moon, planets).

The Day Sky

The day sky is light. You may see clouds, birds, and the Sun. Airplanes and hot-air balloons may move across the sky. You might see a kite in the air.

an eagle in the day sky

The **Sun** is the brightest space object in the day sky. It warms the land, water, and air on Earth. The Sun makes the sky so bright that you cannot see other stars in the day.

▶ **MAIN IDEA** Name some objects you can see in the day sky.

Sun and clouds ▲

Sometimes you can see the Moon in the day sky. ▼

The Night Sky

The night sky is dark because there is no light from the Sun. You can see the Moon and stars at night. A **star** is a space object that makes its own light.

Sometimes you can see planets. A **planet** is a space object that moves around the Sun. Earth is a planet. Stars and planets look small because they are far away.

▶ **COMPARE AND CONTRAST** How are the day sky and the night sky different?

1 Vocabulary What makes the day sky bright?

2 Reading Skill Tell one way that the Sun and the Moon are alike. Tell one way that they are different.

3 Observe Tell what you see in the sky.

 **Technology** Visit **www.eduplace.com/scp/** to find out more about day and night.

What Causes Day and Night?

Science and You

Knowing how Earth moves helps you understand day and night.

Inquiry Skill

Infer Use what you observe and know to tell what you think.

STANDARDS
SC.H.1.1.3.1.1. works with others to complete an experiment or to solve a problem.

What You Need

school picture

tape

flashlight

Day and Night

Steps

1. **Use Models** Tape your school picture on your clothes. The picture stands for your school on Earth.

2. **Infer** Have a partner shine a flashlight on the picture. The flashlight is the Sun. Tell whether it is day or night at school.

3. Turn until your school faces away from the Sun's light. Observe whether it is day or night.

Think and Share

1. When was it day at school? When was it night?

2. **Predict** What will happen if you keep turning? Try it.

Investigate More!

Experiment Mark on a globe where you live. Then use a flashlight and turn the globe to model day and night where you live.

Day on Earth

Earth **rotates**, or spins. As Earth rotates, the Sun shines on different parts of it. It is day when the part of Earth where you live faces the Sun. The sky is light.

▶ **CAUSE AND EFFECT** Why is the sky light during the day?

It is easier to see outside during the day.

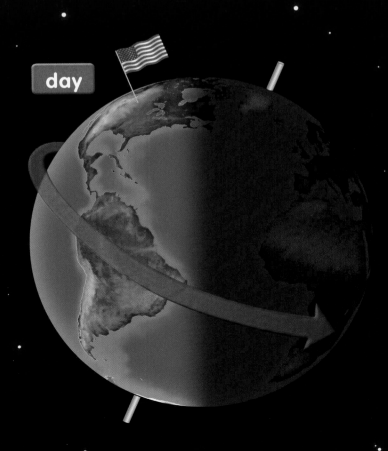

day

Night on Earth

It is night when the part of Earth where you live faces away from the Sun. The sky is dark.

It takes 24 hours for Earth to rotate one time. Earth keeps rotating. Day and night repeat.

▶ **CAUSE AND EFFECT** Why is the sky dark at night?

night

You need lights
to see at night.

Lesson Wrap-Up

❶ **Vocabulary** How does Earth move when it **rotates**?

❷ **Reading Skill** What causes day on Earth?

❸ **Infer** If it is night where you are, where do you think it is day?

🔦 **Technology** Visit **www.eduplace.com/scp/** to find out more about Earth's rotation.

How Does the Moon Seem to Change?

Science and You

Knowing how the Moon changes can help you understand the night sky.

Inquiry Skill

Use Models Use a model to find how the Moon seems to change.

 STANDARDS
SC.H.1.1.3.1.1. works with others to complete an experiment or to solve a problem.

What You Need

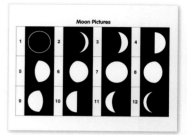

Moon pictures

scissors

stapler

Moon Changes

Steps

1. Cut out Moon pictures.
   Safety: Scissors are sharp!

STEP 1

2. **Use Numbers** Pile the pictures in order from 1 to 12. Staple the pictures together to make a book.

STEP 2

3. **Use Models** Hold one side of the book in one hand. Flip the pages with your other hand.

STEP 3

Think and Share

1. What did you observe about the Moon when you flipped the pages?

2. What do you think your model shows about the real Moon?

Investigate More!

Experiment How can you predict what the Moon will look like on a cloudy night? Make a plan to find out. Tell how your plan works.

VocabularyFCAT

Moon

Reading Skill

Sequence

STANDARDS
SC.E.1.1.1.1.1. knows that the amount of light reflected by the Moon is a little different every day but the Moon appears the same again about every 28 days.

The Moon

The **Moon** is a space object close to Earth. From Earth you can see dark spots on the Moon. Some spots are pits called craters.

Astronauts have visited the Moon.

The Sun is a star that makes its own light. The Moon is not a star. It does not make its own light. We see the part of the Moon that the Sun is shining on.

▶ **CAUSE AND EFFECT** Why does the Moon seem bright?

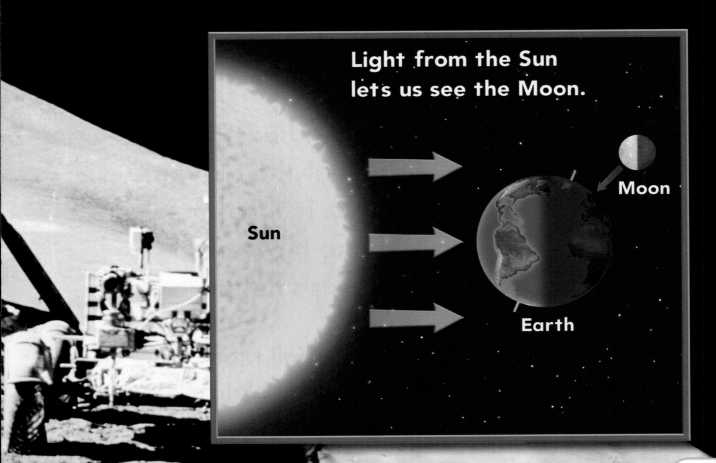

Light from the Sun lets us see the Moon.

Sun

Moon

Earth

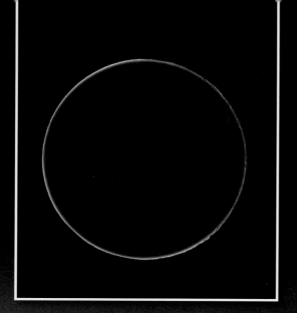

new Moon

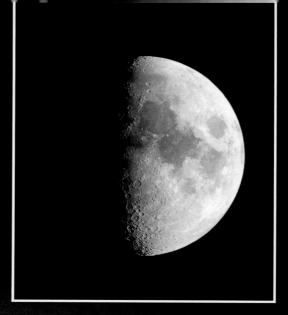

first quarter Moon

The Changing Moon

The Moon's shape looks different every night. The Moon is round, but we may not see all of it.

The Moon moves around Earth. We see different parts of the Moon's lighted side as it moves. It takes about 28 days for the Moon to move around Earth. Then it looks the same again.

▶ **SEQUENCE** If there is a full Moon tonight, what will the Moon look like after 28 days?

full Moon

last quarter Moon

Lesson Wrap-Up

① **Vocabulary** How is the **Moon** different from the Sun?

② **Reading Skill** How does the Moon seem to change?

③ **Use Models** How can a model show how the Moon changes?

Technology Visit **www.eduplace.com/scp/** to find out more about the Moon.

Neil Armstrong
Astronaut

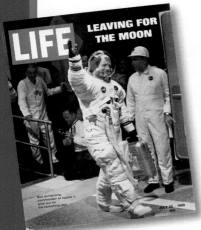

Neil Armstrong was the commander of the Apollo 11 space mission. On July 16, 1969, the Apollo crew took off from Kennedy Space Center in Florida.

Neil Armstrong was the first person to step onto the Moon. He and astronaut Buzz Aldrin collected Moon rocks so they could find out what the Moon is made of.

Neil Armstrong walks on the Moon!

July 16, 1969
Apollo 11 launches from
Kennedy Space Center,
Florida

Sharing Ideas

1. **Write About It** Why did Neil Armstrong collect Moon rocks?

2. **Talk About It** If you were an astronaut, where in space would you want to go?

How Does the Sun Seem to Move?

Science and You

You can check your shadow to guess the time of day.

Inquiry Skill

Predict Use what you know to tell what you think might happen.

STANDARDS
SC.H.2.1.1.1.1. uses information gathered to identify patterns in nature to make predictions (for example, shapes of leaves, petals on flowers, rings on seashells).

What You Need

crayons

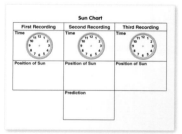

Sun chart

clock

Sun Changes

Steps

1. **Observe** Go outdoors in the morning. Find where the Sun is in the sky. **Safety:** Do not look right at the Sun!

STEP 1

2. **Record Data** Use a chart to show where the Sun is. Go out at noon. Record what you find.

STEP 2

Sun Chart		
First Recording	**Second Recording**	**Third Recording**
Time	Time	Time
Position of Sun	Position of Sun	Position of Sun
low	Prediction	

3. **Predict** Look at your data. Predict where the Sun will be next. Check your prediction.

STEP 3

Think and Share

1. What did you observe about the Sun?

2. How did your prediction compare to what happened?

Investigate More!

Experiment Make a plan to observe how the Sun changes shadows during the day. Talk with the class about what you learn.

Vocabulary

shadow

Reading Skill
Draw
Conclusions

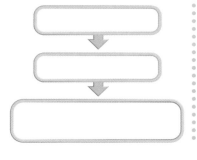

STANDARDS
SC.E.1.1.2.1.1. knows that day and night
are caused by the rotation of the Earth.

The Sun

The Sun seems to move from one side of the sky to the other. The Sun is low in the sky in the morning. It is higher in the sky at noon. The Sun is low in the sky late in the day.

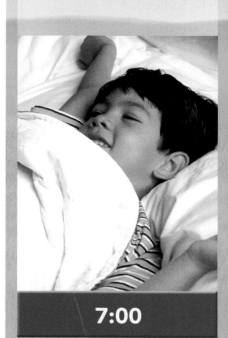

7:00

9:00

The Sun is not moving. Earth is moving. As Earth rotates, we see the Sun, Moon, or stars in different parts of the sky.

▶ **DRAW CONCLUSIONS** Where is the Sun when you eat breakfast?

12:00

3:00

5:00

The Sun and Shadows

A **shadow** forms when an object blocks light. Shadows change during the day because the Sun is in different parts of the sky.

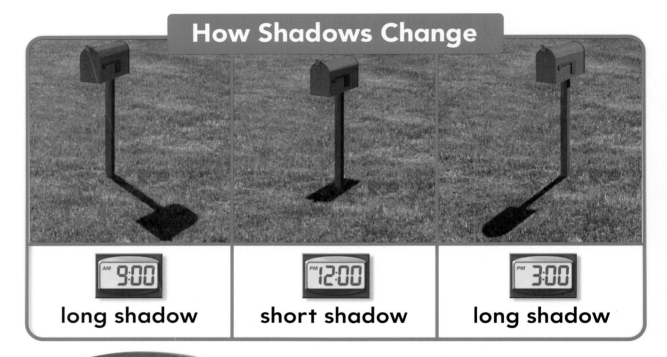

How Shadows Change

AM 9:00	PM 12:00	PM 3:00
long shadow	short shadow	long shadow

Lesson Wrap-Up

❶ **Vocabulary** How does a **shadow** form?

❷ **Reading Skill** What happens to the Sun in the sky as Earth rotates?

❸ **Predict** Will the shadow of a tree be long or short at 4 o'clock?

Technology Visit **www.eduplace.com/scp/** to find out more about the Sun.

Math Measure Shadows

Work with a partner. Measure each others' shadows many times during the day. Measure from your foot to the end of the shadow. Record what you observe. Tell how your shadow changed.

My Shadow		
Time of Day	Where the Sun Is	Length of Shadow
_____ o'clock	high in the sky low in the sky	_____ feet
_____ o'clock	high in the sky low in the sky	_____ feet
_____ o'clock	high in the sky low in the sky	_____ feet

Language Arts Write a Story

Think about what you see in the day sky or the night sky. Write a story about what you see.

Visual Summary

Day and night happen when Earth rotates.

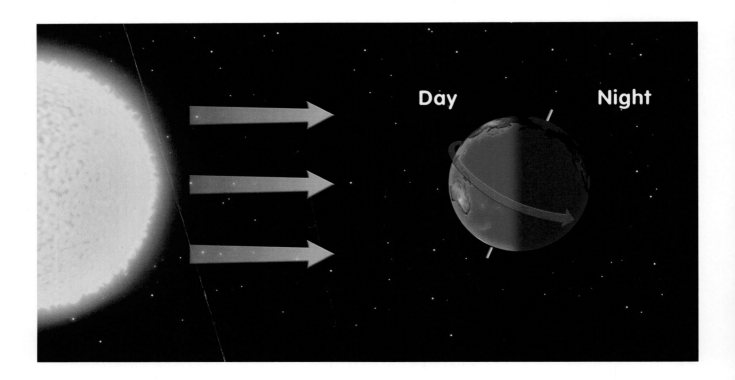

Day   Night

Main Ideas

1. What can you see in the day sky? (pp. D46–D47)

2. What can you see in the night sky? (p. D48)

3. What causes day and night? (pp. D52–D55)

4. Draw pictures to show four different ways the Moon can look. (pp. D60–D61)

Vocabulary and Science Skills

Choose the correct answer.

5. Which shines on the moon?

○ Earth   ○ the planets   ○ the Sun

6. Shadows form when objects block ____.

○ time   ○ light   ○ planets

7. A round, bright moon is a ____.

○ new Moon   ○ full Moon
○ last quarter Moon

8. Which warms land and water on Earth?

○ shadows   ○ the Sun   ○ the Moon

9. What causes day and night?

○ Earth rotates.   ○ The Sun moves.
○ The Moon changes.

10. Why do you not see stars in the day?

○ The stars are gone.   ○ The Sun is bright.
○ The Moon is round.

Discover!

Where are the stars during the day?

Stars are always in the sky. During the day, the Sun makes the sky too bright to see other stars. At night, the Sun does not shine on your part of Earth. Then you can see the light from other stars.

Go to **www.eduplace.com/scp/** to find the stars during the day.

Describing Matter

Boats of Florida

Houseboat

Used by: Residents of Florida

Where: Florida rivers and lakes

Boats are: 20 to 65 feet long

Fun fact: they are like houses that float on water

Shrimp Boat

Used by: fishers

Where: the Keys, St. Petersburg, Tampa

Boats at work: 853

Fun fact: Florida boats bring in 11,509 tons of shrimp in one year

Cruise Ship

Used by: travelers

Where: Miami

Boats travel to: Europe, the Caribbean, Asia

Fun fact: more than 90,000 people work with these ships

Airboat

Used by: tourists

Where: Everglades

Boats can: float over shallow water

Fun fact: powered by air; can go 40 miles per hour

PHYSICAL UNIT E SCIENCE

Describing Matter

Reading in Science.............. E2

Chapter 10
Observing Objects.............. E4

Chapter 11
Changes in Matter........... E34

Independent Reading

Sink or Float

Louis Braille

Balloons

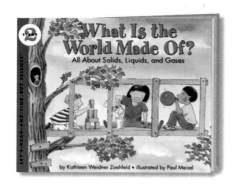

What Is the World Made Of?

by Kathleen Weidner Zoehfeld
illustrated by Paul Meisel

Walls and blocks, dolls and socks. Milk and lemonade. Rocks and trees. All of these things are made of matter.

The air in the breeze that blows the leaves. Water flowing in the creek. Everything on earth is made of matter.

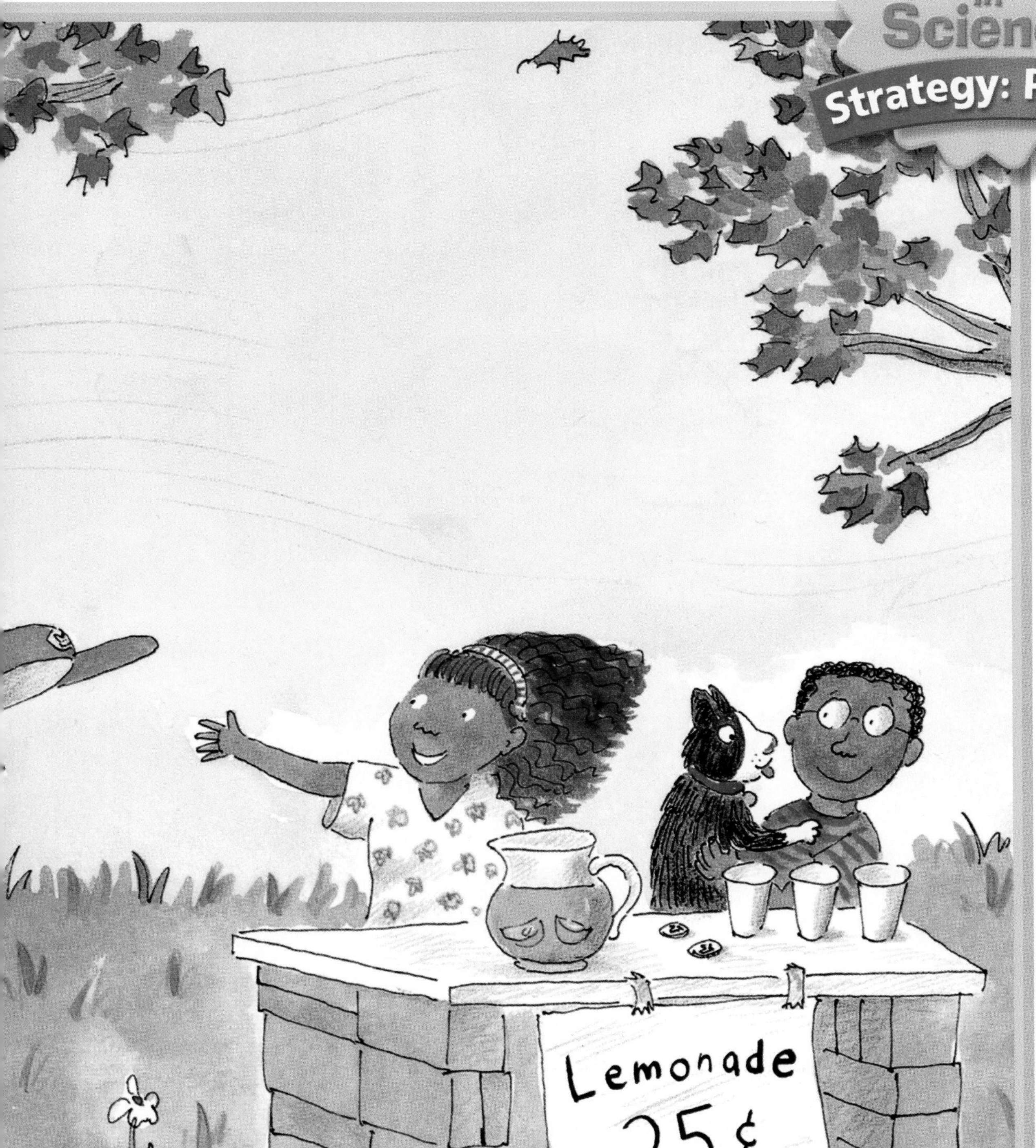
Lemonade
25¢

Chapter 10

Observing Objects

matter

property

magnify

weigh

magnet

attracts

repel

sink

float

matter

Matter is what all things are made of.

magnify

To magnify is to make something look larger.

magnet

A magnet is an object that pulls iron and steel toward it.

sink

To sink is to drop to the bottom of water.

How Can You Describe Matter?

Science and You

Your senses tell you about objects around you.

Inquiry Skill

Classify You can use your senses to group objects that are alike.

What You Need

objects

index cards

marker

STANDARDS
SC.H.1.1.3.1.2. listens, records, and compares the ideas and observations of others.

Classify Objects

Steps

1. **Classify** Decide how the objects are alike. Sort them into groups.

2. **Record Data** Name your groups. Write the name of each group on a different card.

3. **Communicate** Tell how the objects in each group are alike. Write your ideas on the cards.

Think and Share

1. How did you sort the objects?

2. Why might one person's ideas about sorting be different from another person's?

Investigate More!

Work Together Work with a partner. Talk about other ways to sort the objects. How many groups can you make?

E7

▶ **Vocabulary**FCAT

matter

property

▶ **Reading Skill**
Main Idea and
Details

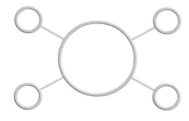

STANDARDS
SC.A.1.1.1.1.1. knows that objects can
be grouped according to their physical
characteristics (for example, shape, color,
texture, form, size).

Matter and Your Senses

Matter is what all things are made of. People use their senses to learn about matter. Sight, smell, hearing, touch, and taste are senses. You see and smell a flower. Many flowers have pleasant smells. You feel a kitten's fur. It is soft.

You can see, smell, touch, and taste your lunch.

You can use your senses to compare these dogs.

Comparing Dogs

Sense	Dog A	Dog B
Hearing	low sound	high sound
Sight	large and brown	small and white
Touch	smooth	rough

▶ **MAIN IDEA** What can your senses tell you about different things?

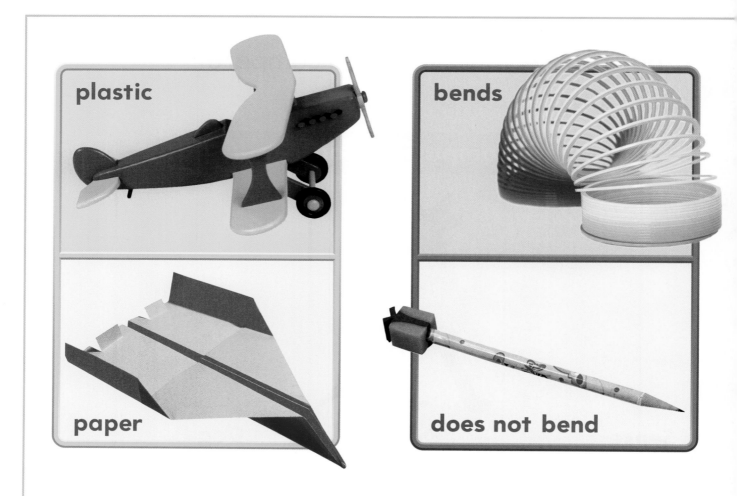

plastic

bends

paper

does not bend

Observing Properties

You can use your senses to describe a property of an object. A **property** is anything that you learn about an object by using your senses. You can see an object's size, shape, and color. You can see what it is made of. You can tell how it sounds, smells, and tastes.

sweet

sour

soft

hard

▶ **MAIN IDEA** How can you tell about the properties of an object?

Lesson Wrap-Up

❶ **Vocabulary** What is a **property**?

❷ **Reading Skill** How can your senses help you compare objects?

❸ **Classify** How could you group these objects?

Technology Visit **www.eduplace.com/scp/** to find out more about matter.

How Can You Use Tools to Observe?

Science and You

Using tools can help you compare objects.

Inquiry Skill

Measure Use a tool to find out how much or how many.

STANDARDS
SC.H.1.1.5.1.1. uses a variety of tools (for example, thermometers, magnifiers, rulers, scales, computers) to identify characteristics of objects.

What You Need

objects

balance

hand lens

ruler

Use Tools

Steps

STEP 1

1. **Measure** Use a ruler to measure an object. Tell what you find.

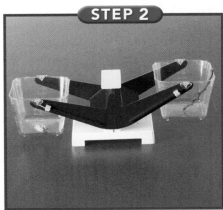

STEP 2

2. **Compare** Use a balance to compare the weights of two objects. Tell what you find.

STEP 3

3. **Observe** Use a hand lens to look closely at one of the objects. Tell what you see.

Think and Share

1. What did you learn about each object?

2. How did the tools help you?

Investigate More!

Solve a Problem

Everyone in art class wants clay. How can you use a tool to make sure each child gets the same amount?

Vocabulary

magnify

weigh

Reading Skill
Main Idea and Details

STANDARDS

SC.A.2.1.1.1.1. knows that objects are composed of parts that are too small to be seen without magnification (for example, rocks, cookies, string, paper).
SC.H.3.1.1.1.1. knows that scientists and technologists use a variety of tools (e.g., thermometers, magnifiers, rulers, and scales) to obtain information in more detail and to make work easier.

How can a hand lens help this girl learn about the properties of a ladybug?

A Tool to Magnify

Scientists use tools to learn about the properties of matter. You can use tools, too.

A hand lens can magnify an object. To **magnify** is to make something look larger.

without a hand lens

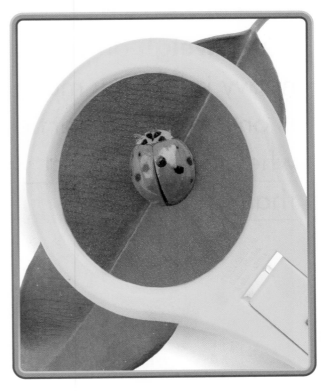

with a hand lens

Objects look different when you look at them with a hand lens. You can see tiny parts that you cannot see without a hands lens.

▶ **MAIN IDEA** How can a hand lens help you observe an object?

A Tool to Weigh

You **weigh** an object to find how heavy it is. How much an object weighs is one of its properties. A balance tells whether one object weighs more than another.

The balance is lower on the side with the blue toy because the blue toy weighs more than the orange toy.

Tools for Length

You can use rulers or measuring tapes to find how long or tall objects are. You also can measure with things such as paper clips or your fingers.

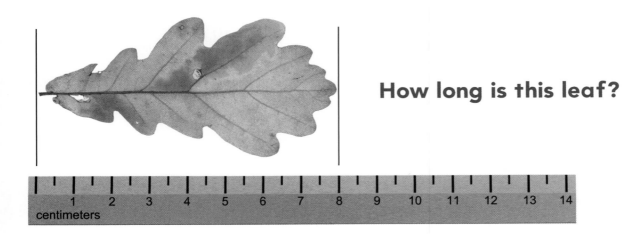

How long is this leaf?

centimeters

▶ **MAIN IDEA** What tool tells you which object weighs more than another?

Lesson Wrap-Up

❶ **Vocabulary** What does **magnify** mean?

❷ **Reading Skill** What tools can you use to learn about the properties of matter?

❸ **Measure** Which tool measures length?

Technology visit **www.eduplace.com/scp/** to find out more about tools.

What Does a Magnet Attract?

Science and You

People use magnets to pick up objects and to hold things.

Inquiry Skill

Infer Use what you observe and know to tell what you think.

STANDARDS
SC.H.1.1.5.1.1. uses a variety of tools (for example, thermometers, magnifiers, rulers, scales, computers) to identify characteristics of objects.

What You Need

magnet

objects

Object	Magnet Pulls	Magnet Does Not Pull

magnet chart

Use Magnets

Steps

1. **Observe** Test each object with a magnet.

2. **Record Data** Decide whether the magnet pulls the object. Record your results.

3. **Compare** Tell how the objects that were pulled and not pulled to the magnet are different.

STEP 1

STEP 2

Object	Magnet Pulls	Magnet Does Not Pull
paper		✓

Think and Share

1. **Infer** What is the same about the objects that the magnet pulled?

2. **Predict** Think of an object that you did not test. Do you think the magnet will pull it? Why or why not?

STEP 3

Investigate More!

Experiment Will a magnet attract an object if there is something between the magnet and the object? Make a plan for finding an answer.

▶ **Vocabulary** FCAT ◥

magnet

attracts

repel

▶ **Reading Skill**
Cause and
Effect

STANDARDS
SC.A.1.1.1.1.1. knows that objects
can be grouped according to their
physical characteristics (for example,
shape, color, texture, form, size).

**Which materials does
the magnet attract?**

Magnets

A **magnet** is an object that pulls iron and steel toward it. A magnet **attracts** objects when it pulls them. Sometimes a magnet attracts things without touching them. A magnet does not attract everything. It will not attract paper, wood, or plastic objects.

If a magnet attracts an object, you can say that is a property of the object. It is another way to describe the object.

▶ **MAIN IDEA** What does a magnet attract?

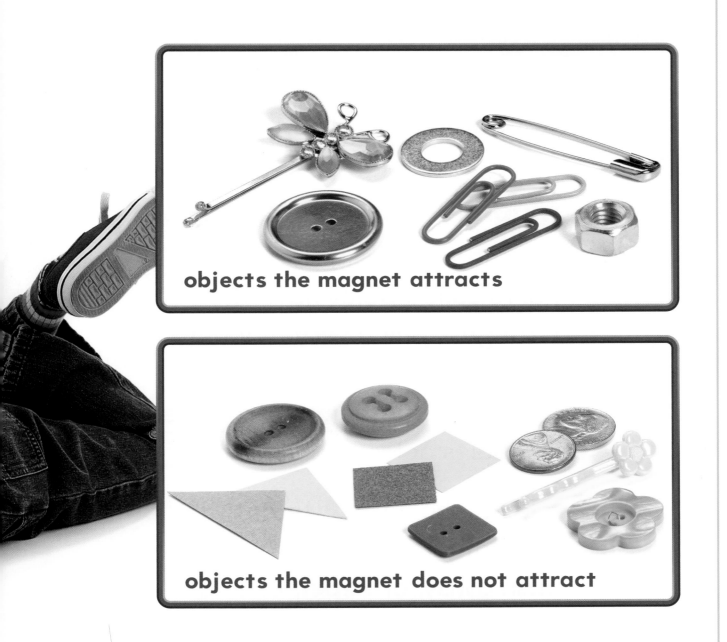

objects the magnet attracts

objects the magnet does not attract

These magnets have different poles next to each other.

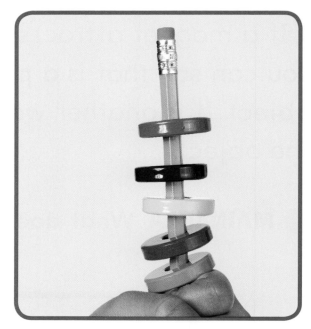

These magnets have poles that are alike next to each other.

Magnets Act on Each Other

A magnet has different parts. Parts called poles have the strongest pull. Every magnet has two poles. When you put two magnets together, you can feel the poles act on each other.

Poles that are different attract each other. Poles that are alike push away, or **repel**, each other.

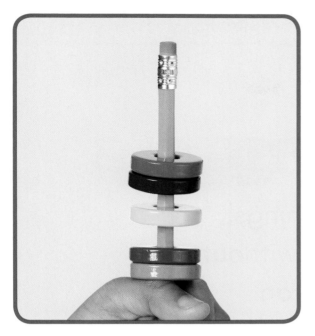 

Are the poles next to each
other alike or different?

▶ **CAUSE AND EFFECT** What causes
magnets to repel each other?

Lesson Wrap-Up

❶ **Vocabulary** How do magnets act when
they **repel** each other?

❷ **Reading Skill** Why are some objects
attracted by a magnet?

❸ **Infer** Part of one magnet pulls part of
another magnet. What can you infer about
the two parts of the magnets?

Technology Visit **www.eduplace.com/scp**
to find out more about magnets.

Mighty Magnets

Magnets are interesting things. They can attract objects without touching them. Magnets can even attract objects if there is something between the magnet and the object.

The sled has metal on it. The magnet can move the sled without touching it.

The fish has steel on its mouth. The magnet on the fishing pole attracts the fish through water. ▶

◀ There are tiny pieces of iron in the bag. When the magnet moves, the iron makes different patterns.

Sharing Ideas

1. **Write About It** Use your own words to write about ways that magnets attract objects.

2. **Talk About It** What are some other ways that magnets could be used?

E25

What Floats and What Sinks?

Science and You

When you go swimming, it is good to know what things float.

Inquiry Skill

Predict Use what you know to tell what will happen.

 STANDARDS
SC.H.1.1.4.1.1. uses simple graphs, pictures, written statements, and numbers to observe, describe, record, and compare data.

What You Need

tub

water

objects

Float-and-Sink Chart		
Object	Prediction	What Happened?
	float sink	floated sank
	float sink	floated sank
	float sink	floated sank
	float sink	floated sank
	float sink	floated sank
	float sink	floated sank
	float sink	floated sank
	float sink	floated sank

float-and-sink chart

Float or Sink

Steps

① Pour water into a tub.

② **Predict** Choose an object. Decide if it will float or sink. Write your prediction.

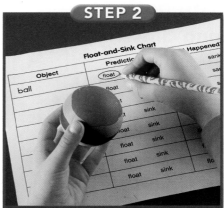

③ **Observe** Put the object in the water. Watch what happens.

④ **Record Data** Write what happened. Test other objects.

Think and Share

1. Compare your prediction with what you observed.

2. **Infer** What is the same about the objects that floated?

Investigate More!

Experiment Take a ball of clay. Change its shape to make it float. Draw the shape you made.

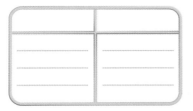

🌴 **STANDARDS**
SC.A.1.1.1.1.1. knows that objects can be grouped according to their physical characteristics (for example, shape, color, texture, form, size).

Floating and Sinking

Some objects **sink**, or drop to the bottom of water. Other objects **float**, or stay on top of water. Floating and sinking are properties of an object. You can group objects that float. You can also group objects that sink.

Which objects float?
Which objects sink?

Sometimes the weight of an object helps it float. Light objects often float. Sometimes the shape of an object helps it float. Flat objects often float. Sometimes objects float because they have air in them.

▶ **CLASSIFY** **What are some objects that float?**

Making Objects Sink

You can cause some floating objects to sink. Sometimes you can make an object sink by changing its shape or filling it with water.

The cup sinks when it fills with water.

Lesson Wrap-Up

❶ Vocabulary What does **float** mean?

❷ Reading Skill Name two things that sink.

❸ Predict Look at these objects. Which one is likely to float? Tell why.

 Technology Visit **www.eduplace.com/scp/** to find out more about floating and sinking.

L I N K S
for Home and School

Math **Read a Bar Graph**

Bob dipped different magnets into a pile of paper clips. The graph shows the number of paper clips each magnet attracted.

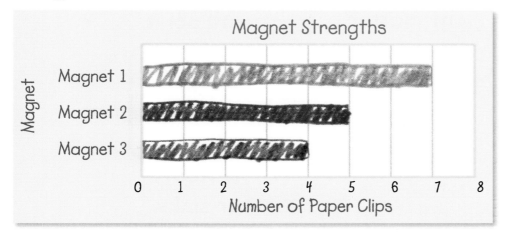

Magnet Strengths

1. How many paper clips did each magnet attract?

2. What is the difference in the number of paper clips for magnets 1 and 3?

Language Arts **Write a Letter**

Write a letter to a friend about your favorite food. Tell how the food looks, tastes, feels, sounds, and smells.

Visual Summary

Matter has many properties.

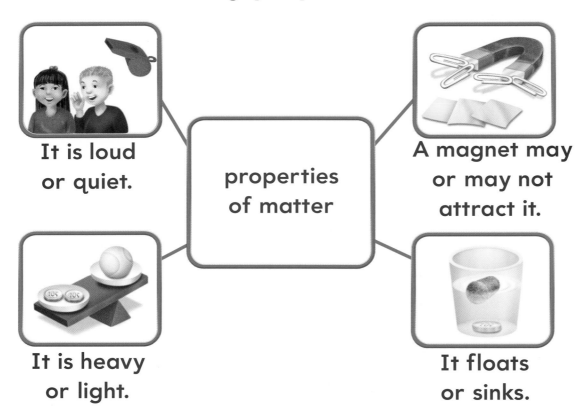

It is loud or quiet.

properties of matter

A magnet may or may not attract it.

It is heavy or light.

It floats or sinks.

Main Ideas

1. What are an object's properties? **(p. E10)**

2. What does a balance tell you? **(p. E16)**

3. Two objects push away from each other. Use another word to tell how the magnets act. **(p. E22)**

4. Why do some things sink? **(p. E29)**

Vocabulary and Science Skills

Choose the correct answer.

5. All things are made of ____.

○ senses   ○ matter   ○ property

6. Which can magnify an object?

○ hand lens   ○ ruler   ○ balance

7. Which attracts iron and steel?

○ ruler   ○ wood   ○ magnet

8. Sight is one of your ____.

○ objects   ○ senses   ○ tools

9. Which is likely to sink?

○ toy boat   ○ marble   ○ leaf

10. Different poles on magnets ____ each other.

○ repel   ○ attract   ○ float

Chapter 11

Changes in Matter

solid

liquid

gas

freeze

melt

evaporate

mixture

dissolve

solid

A solid is matter that has its own shape.

liquid

A liquid is matter that flows and takes the shape of its container.

gas

A gas is matter that changes shape to fill all the space it is in.

melt

To melt is to change from a solid to a liquid.

What Are Solids, Liquids, and Gases?

Science and You

Water can spill because it is a liquid.

Inquiry Skill

Compare Look carefully to see how objects are alike or different.

STANDARDS
SC.H.1.1.3.1.1. works with others to complete an experiment or to solve a problem.

What You Need

containers

colored water

rock

balloon

Compare Matter

Steps

1. **Observe** Gently squeeze a balloon. Tell what happens to the shape.

2. **Compare** Squeeze a rock. Put it in each container. Tell what happens to the shape of the rock.

3. **Communicate** Pour water into each container. Tell what happens to the shape of the water.

STEP 1

STEP 2

STEP 3

Think and Share

1. What happened when you squeezed the balloon?

2. Compare the rock and the water in the containers. How were they different?

Investigate More!

Solve a Problem Suppose you want to send one of the objects to someone who lives far away. Which object would be easiest to pack? Why?

▶ **Reading Skill**

Categorize and Classify

🏴 **STANDARDS**
SC.A.1.1.1.1.1. knows that objects can be grouped according to their physical characteristics (for example, shape, color, texture, form, size).
SC.D.1.1.1.1.1. extends and refines knowledge that the surface of the Earth is composed of different types of solid materials.

Solids

Matter is what all things are made of. Three forms of matter are solids, liquids, and gases. A **solid** is matter that has its own shape. Rocks and soil are solids. Objects in your room are solids, too.

A solid keeps its shape unless you do something to change it. You can cut, tear, bend, or break a solid to change its shape.

▶ **CLASSIFY** **What are three things that are solids?**

What solids do you see in this picture?

Liquids

You can pour water. You can pour milk and juice. Water, milk, and juice are liquids. A **liquid** is matter that flows and takes the shape of its container. A liquid does not have its own shape. It does not always fill its container.

▼ How can you change the shape of a liquid?

Gases

The air around you is a gas. A **gas** is matter that changes shape to fill all the space it is in.

▼ A gas spreads out to fill a balloon.

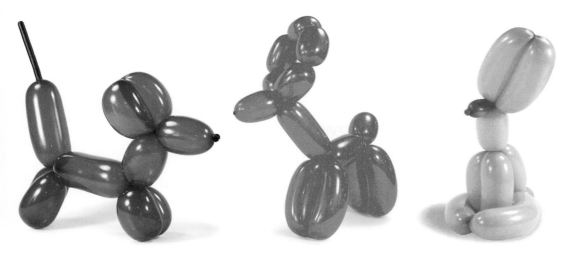

▶ **CLASSIFY** What forms of matter do not have their own shape?

Lesson Wrap-Up

❶ **Vocabulary** What is a **liquid**?

❷ **Reading Skill** What form of matter are milk, juice, and water?

❸ **Compare** How are solids, liquids, and gases different?

Technology Visit **www.eduplace.com/scp/** to find out more about matter.

What Do Heating and Cooling Do?

Science and You

Snow melts when it is heated.

Inquiry Skill

Predict Use what you know to tell what you think will happen.

STANDARDS
SC.H.1.1.3.1.2. listens, records, and compares the ideas and observations of others.

What You Need

bags of ice

warm and cold water

timer

Predict Changes

Steps

1. Put one bag of ice in a bowl of cold water. Put the other bag of ice in a bowl of warm water.

2. **Predict** Record what you think will happen to the ice in each bowl.

3. **Observe** Wait five minutes. Look to see how the ice cubes changed.

STEP 1

STEP 2

STEP 3

Think and Share

1. **Communicate** Tell others how the ice changed.

2. **Infer** Why did the bags of ice change in different ways?

Investigate More!

Experiment How can you make the water change back into a solid? Think of a plan for finding an answer. Then test your plan.

Vocabulary FCAT

freeze

melt

evaporate

Reading Skill

Cause and Effect

STANDARDS
SC.A.1.1.2.1.1. knows the effects of heating and cooling on solids, liquids and gases.
SC.A.1.1.3.1.1. knows the physical properties of ice, water, and steam.

Water Changes

Water on Earth can change from one form to another. Water freezes when it gets very cold. To **freeze** is to change from a liquid to a solid. Ice is solid water. You freeze water to make ice cubes.

Some solids melt when they are heated. To **melt** is to change from a solid to a liquid. When ice gets warm, it melts. A frozen pond melts in spring.

Juice changes from a liquid to a solid when it freezes. It changes from a solid back to a liquid when it melts.

Fall
The water in the pond is liquid.

Winter
The water on the top of the pond is solid.

Spring
The water in the pond is liquid again.

▶ **CAUSE AND EFFECT** What causes the pond to change from season to season?

Liquid to Gas

Water on Earth can be a gas, too. <u>Water evaporates when it is heated.</u> To **evaporate** is to change from a liquid to a gas. You cannot see water when it is a gas.

▶ **CAUSE AND EFFECT** What causes water to change into a gas?

Heat from the Sun made the puddles evaporate.

Lesson Wrap-Up

❶ **Vocabulary** What happens when water **evaporates**?

❷ **Reading Skill** What causes liquid water to change into ice?

❸ **Predict** Look at this picture. What will happen to the liquid water? Why?

⌨ **Technology** Visit **www.eduplace.com/scp/** to find out more about water changing form.

Focus On Florida

Literature

STANDARDS
SC.A.1.1.2.1.1. knows the effects of heating and cooling on solids, liquids, and gases.

READING LINK

Read to find out about cold weather in warm places.

Big Freeze

by Catherine Chambers

Florida is usually warm for most of the year. When it suddenly gets cold there, people, plants, and animals may not be ready. They can be harmed by the cold. This is a big freeze.

Wild Weather

Big Freeze

Sharing Ideas

1. **Write About It** Why do farmers in Florida worry about a big freeze?

2. **Talk About It** How would you stay safe during a big freeze?

What Happens When You Mix Things?

Science and You

You make a mixture when you put fruit and milk on cereal.

Inquiry Skill

Observe Use your senses to help you understand something that happens.

STANDARDS
SC.H.1.1.3.1.1. works with others to complete an experiment or to solve a problem.

What You Need

bowl

spoon

warm water

salt

Make a Mixture

Steps

1. **Predict** Put salt in a bowl. Add water to the bowl. Tell what you think will happen when you stir the mixture.

2. Stir. Tell how the mixture looks. **Safety:** Do not taste the mixture!

3. **Observe** Put the mixture in a warm place. Look at what happens after a few days.

STEP 1

STEP 2

STEP 3

Think and Share

1. How does your prediction compare to what happens?

2. **Communicate** Tell what you learned about the mixture.

Investigate More!

Work Together Try mixing other things with water. You might use solids or other liquids. Share what you observe.

Learn by Reading

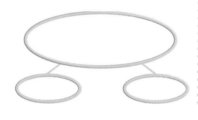

Vocabulary FCAT

mixture

dissolve

Reading Skill

Main Idea and Details

STANDARDS

SC.A.1.1.1.1.1. knows that objects can be grouped according to their physical characteristics (for example, shape, color, texture, form, size).

Solid Mixtures

A **mixture** is two or more kinds of matter put together. Some mixtures are all solids. You have a mixture when you make a sandwich.

What are the solids that make up this mixture?

Mixtures can be taken apart. You can take parts off your sandwich. You can use a magnet to pull iron or steel from some mixtures. You can even use a screen to sift out the small parts of a mixture.

▶ **MAIN IDEA** **How can you make a mixture?**

Mixing Solids and Liquids

You can make a mixture with solids and liquids. Some solids **dissolve**, or mix completely, in water. Sugar dissolves in water. You cannot see it, but it is there.

◄ **A drink mix dissolves in water.**

Lesson Wrap-Up

❶ **Vocabulary** What is a **mixture**?

❷ **Reading Skill** Are toys in a toy box a mixture? Tell why or why not.

❸ **Observe** What are different ways a mixture can look?

🖥 **Technology** Visit **www.eduplace.com/scp/** to find out more about mixtures.

LINKS for Home and School

Math Write Number Sentences

Mix 10 buttons and 10 marbles.
Take out a handful of the mixture.

$$4+2=6$$
$$4-2=2$$

1. How many buttons and marbles did you take out?

2. Which kind of object do you have more of? How many more?

Art Sand Paintings

Native Americans tell stories with sand paintings. They mix many colors of sand. Use sand, rocks, or other solids to make a picture that tells a story.

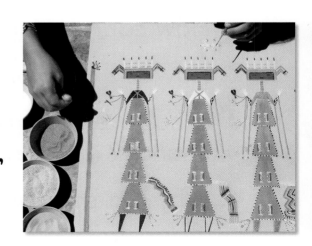

Visual Summary

Matter has different forms.

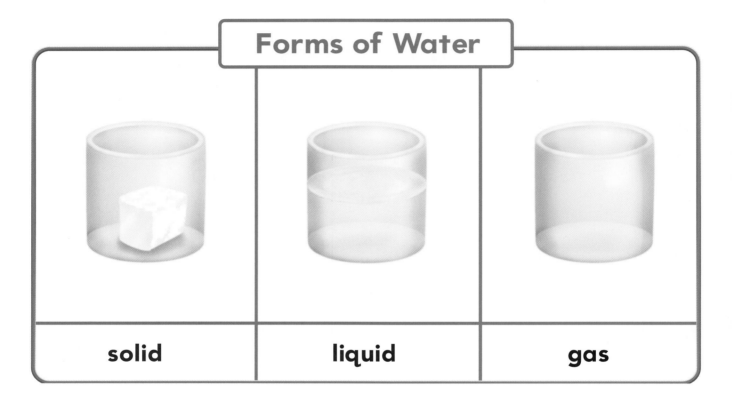

Forms of Water

| solid | liquid | gas |

Main Ideas

1. How can you tell if an object is a solid? **(p. E38)**

2. How are gases and liquids alike? **(pp. E40–E41)**

3. What are three ways that water can change? **(pp. E44–E46)**

4. Why is a sandwich a mixture? **(pp. E50–E51)**

Vocabulary and Science Skills

Choose the correct answer.

5. Which substance is a gas?

○ air   ○ cookies   ○ milk

6. When water changes to a solid, it _____.

○ freezes   ○ melts   ○ evaporates

7. Which has its own shape?

○ solid   ○ liquid   ○ gas

8. When a liquid changes to a gas, it _____.

○ freezes   ○ melts   ○ evaporates

9. Which is a mixture?

○ water   ○ sugar   ○ sandwich

10. Which can dissolve in water?

○ sugar   ○ cheese   ○ bread

Discover!

Will a pumpkin float in water?

A pumpkin has a large center space filled with air and seeds. The air helps the pumpkin float. If you fill that center space with water, the pumpkin will sink a little lower.

Go to **www.eduplace.com/scp/** to test which objects sink and which objects float.

PHYSICAL UNIT F SCIENCE

Energy Sources and Motion

Cricket Connection

Visit www.eduplace.com/scp/ to check out *Click, Ask,* and *Odyssey* magazine articles and activities.

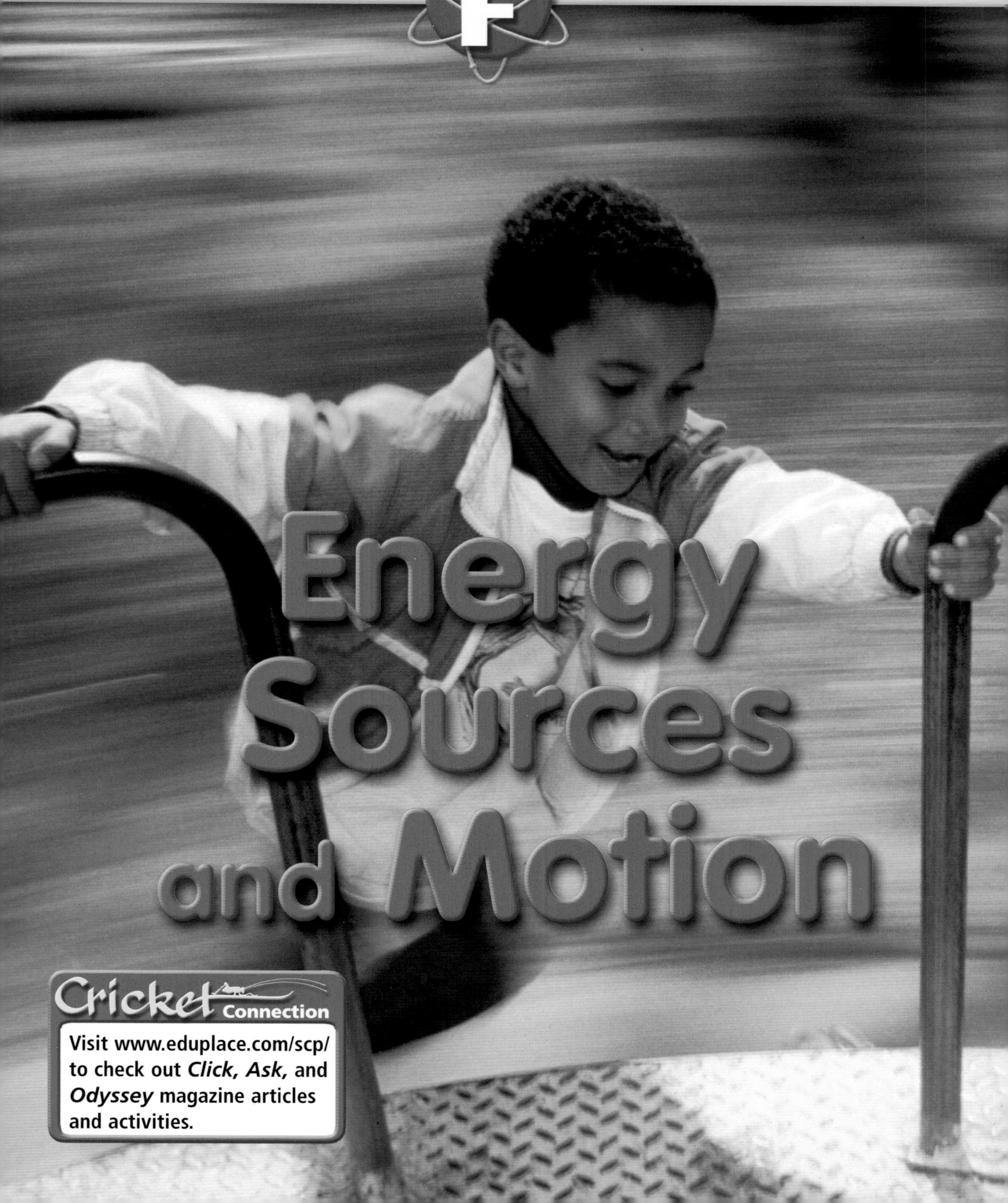

Florida Fun Rides

The Cat in the Hat

Where: Orlando

Cars: 28

Riders: 7 in each car

Fun fact: like a ride through the famous Dr. Seuss story

Mad Tea Party

Where: Orlando

Cars: 18 tea cups

Riders: 4 in each cup

Fun fact: based on Alice in Wonderland's unbirthday party

Silly Sub

Where: Panama City

Cars: one

Riders: must be less than 50 inches tall

Fun fact: has two round windows called portholes

Serengeti Express Railway

Where: Tampa

Cars: one train

Riders: start trip from Nairobi Station

Fun fact: can see animals from Africa

Sunshine State Standards

SC.A.1.1.2.1.1. knows the effects of heating and cooling on solids, liquids, and gases.

SC.B.1.1.1.1.1. knows that heat from the Sun has varying effects depending on the surface it strikes.

SC.B.1.1.2.1.1. predicts which materials will allow light to pass through and which ones will not.

SC.B.1.1.4.1.1. knows ways that human activities require and release energy.

SC.C.1.1.1.1.1. knows the relative order of speeds of various objects (for example, snails, turtles, tricycles, bicycles, cars, jets, rockets).

SC.C.1.1.2.1.1. knows that various things move at different speeds when different forces are applied.

SC.C.2.1.1.1.1. understands various ways gravity affects the motion of objects (for example, an object on a ramp, an object that is dropped).

SC.C.2.1.2.1.1. knows that vibrations of objects (for example, strings, drumheads, rubber bands) cause sounds.

SC.H.1.1.2.1.1. understands the importance of accuracy and repetition in conducting scientific inquiries.

SC.H.1.1.3.1.1. works with others to complete an experiment or to solve a problem.

SC.H.1.1.3.1.2. listens, records, and compares the ideas and observations of others.

SC.H.1.1.4.1.1. uses simple graphs, pictures, written statements, and numbers to observe, describe, record, and compare data.

SC.H.1.1.5.1.1. uses a variety of tools (for example, thermometers, magnifiers, rulers, scales, computers) to identify characteristics of objects.

SC.H.1.1.5.1.2. uses standard (for example, centimeters) and nonstandard units (for example, paper clips, hands, pencils) to measure organisms and objects and parts of organisms and objects.

SC.H.3.1.1.1.1. knows that scientists and technologists use a variety of tools (e.g., thermometers, magnifiers, rulers, and scales) to obtain information in more detail and to make work easier.

Energy Sources and Motion

Reading in Science.............. **F2**

Chapter 12
Heat, Light, and Sound....... **F4**

Chapter 13
**Moving Faster
and Slower**........................ **F32**

Independent Reading

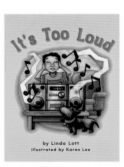

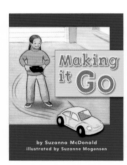

It's Too Loud

Making It Go

Night Lights

What is the fastest a human can run?

Think about this question as you read. You will have the answer by the end of the unit.

Energy
Heat, Light, and Fuel

by Darlene Stille
illustrated by Sheree Boyd

It's morning. You stretch your arms out wide. You jump out of bed. You are full of energy. You use that energy to get things done!

Energy gets lots of things done. There are many forms of energy. Energy heats your house. It lights up lamps. It makes cars, trucks, and buses go.

Chapter 12

Heat, Light, and Sound

energy
heat
light
shadow
sound
vibrates
pitch
volume

heat
Heat is a kind of energy that makes things warm.

light
Light is a kind of energy that you can see.

sound
Sound is a kind of energy that you can hear.

volume
Volume is how loud or soft a sound is.

Where Does Heat Come From?

Science and You

Heat from the Sun can make you hot and thirsty.

Inquiry Skill

Measure You can use a tool to find out how much or how many.

STANDARDS
SC.H.3.1.1.1.1. knows that scientists and technologists use a variety of tools (e.g., thermometers, magnifiers, rulers, and scales) to obtain information in more detail and to make work easier.

What You Need

3 jars

water and sand

3 thermometers

heat chart

Measure Heat

Steps

1. Fill one jar with water. Fill another jar with sand. Leave one jar empty.

STEP 1

2. **Measure** Put a thermometer in each jar. Read each thermometer. Record each temperature.

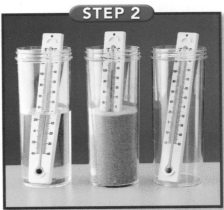

STEP 2

3. **Record Data** Put the jars in a sunny place. Record the temperatures every 30 minutes.

STEP 3

Think and Share

1. **Compare** Which jar had the warmest temperature after 90 minutes?

2. **Infer** Why was one jar warmer?

Investigate More!

Experiment Try the same experiment another day. Is your data the same as it was the first time? Why do you think that happened?

Heat

Energy is something that can cause change or do work. **Heat** is a kind of energy that makes things warm. Earth gets heat from the Sun.

The Sun warms Earth's air, water, and land. The Sun also warms you. You feel warm when you stand in the Sun. You feel cooler when you move to a shady place.

Heat comes from other places, too. Fire gives off heat. So do a lit stove, a burning candle, and a turned-on light bulb. Rubbing things together can make them give off heat, too.

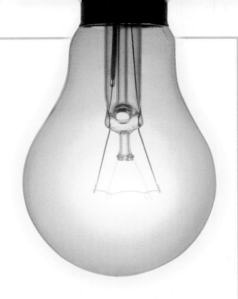

▲ Be careful! Light bulbs get very hot.

▶ **CAUSE AND EFFECT** What warms Earth's air, land, and water?

◀ Heat warms your home.

What happens when you rub your hands together? Try it! ▶

Heat Changes Things

Heat can make things change. Heat from your body makes your sheets warm. Heat from the Sun can make a metal slide too hot to use. Heat from a flame melts a candle. Heat makes butter soft.

▲ Heat makes ice melt.

▼ Heat cooks food.

A fire gives off heat when it burns. You feel the heat as the fire warms your body. Heat spreads out and warms things around it.

Heat can move things. Look at the picture. Heat from the flames moves the air. The air moves the windmill.

▶ **CAUSE AND EFFECT** What are some ways that heat causes change?

Heat can make things move. ▼

Lesson Wrap-Up

❶ **Vocabulary** What is **energy**?

❷ **Reading Skill** How can heat from the Sun or a fire make your body feel different?

❸ **Measure** How could measuring help you find out whether heat has changed the water in a pot on the stove?

Technology Visit **www.eduplace.com/scp/** to find out more about heat.

Where Does Light Come From?

Science and You

A lighthouse helps ships find their way in the dark.

Inquiry Skill

Ask Questions You can ask questions to learn more about the world around you.

STANDARDS
SC.H.1.1.3.1.1. works with others to complete an experiment or to solve a problem.

What You Need

objects

paper

tape

flashlight

Shine Light

Steps

1. Tape paper to a wall. Shine light on the paper.

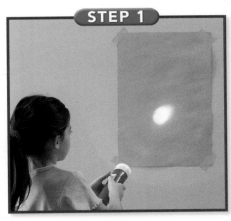
STEP 1

2. **Observe** Hold one object between the flashlight and the paper.

STEP 2

3. **Record Data** Write or draw what you see.

4. **Predict** Tell which objects you think light will pass through. Repeat steps 2 and 3 for each object.

STEP 3

Think and Share

1. How did your predictions compare to what happened?

2. **Classify** Group the objects by how light passes through them. Explain your groups.

Investigate More!

Ask Questions Complete this sentence: I wonder if light will pass through ___. Predict what will happen. Then try it. Share your results.

▶ **Vocabulary** FCAT

light
shadow

▶ **Reading Skill**
Main Idea and Details

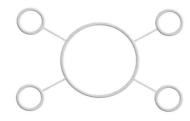

STANDARDS
SC.B.1.1.2.1.1. predicts which
materials will allow light to pass through
and which ones will not.

Light

You know that Earth gets heat from the Sun. Earth also gets light from the Sun. **Light** is a kind of energy that you can see.

Things other than the Sun give off light, too. Fires, candles, and matches are things that burn. They give off light and heat.

The Sun gives off light.

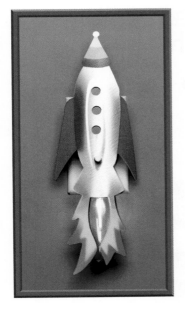

▲ nightlight

▲ fireworks

Light bulbs give off light. When you bend a glow stick, it gives off light. Even some living things give off light.

▶ **MAIN IDEA** What is light?

▲ firefly

Light and Shadows

Light can pass through some things but not others. Light passes through clear glass and clear plastic. It also passes through water and air.

What Light Passes Through

1 Light passes through.

2 Some light passes through.

3 No light passes through.

Other things stop some or all light from passing through. Wax paper and sunglasses block some light. Your body blocks all light. A dark shape called a **shadow** forms when something blocks light.

▶ **MAIN IDEA** What is a shadow?

The boy and the dog block light from the Sun.

Lesson Wrap-Up

❶ **Vocabulary** What kind of energy can you see?

❷ **Reading Skill** What are four things that give off light?

❸ **Ask Questions** What else do you want to know about light and shadows?

💻 **Technology** Visit **www.eduplace.com/scp/** to find out more about light.

How Is Sound Made?

Science and You

Many living things use sound to communicate.

Inquiry Skill

Observe You can look and listen to learn about something.

STANDARDS
SC.H.1.1.4.1.1. uses simple graphs, pictures, written statements, and numbers to observe, describe, record, and compare data.

What You Need

goggles

rubber band

can

Make Sounds

Steps

1. Stretch a rubber band around a can, across the open top. **Safety:** Wear goggles. Hold the rubber band carefully!

STEP 1

2. **Observe** Use your finger to pluck the rubber band. Look and listen closely.

STEP 2

3. **Record Data** Write about what you see and hear.

STEP 3
The rubber band

Think and Share

1. **Compare** How did the rubber band change when you plucked it?

2. **Infer** How do you think sound is made? Tell why.

Investigate More!

Solve a Problem Think of two ways to change the sound the rubber band makes. Then try them. Share your ways with the class.

Vocabulary

sound

vibrates

Reading Skill

Draw
Conclusions

STANDARDS
SC.C.2.1.2.1.1. knows that
vibrations of objects (for example,
strings, drumheads, rubber bands)
cause sounds.

Sound

Sound is a kind of energy that you can hear. Sound is made when something **vibrates**, or moves back and forth very fast. Many kinds of things vibrate and make sound—even you!

The space shuttle makes sound when it blasts off. ▶

You make sound when you talk or sing. Sound happens when moving air makes parts inside your neck vibrate. Place your hand on the side of your neck as you talk. You can feel the parts vibrate.

▲ **Birds make sounds when they sing.**

▶ **DRAW CONCLUSIONS** What causes sound when a bird sings?

▼ **Sound can be music.**

Hearing Sound

A drum vibrates when you strike it. Something that vibrates makes air around it vibrate, too. Air that vibrates makes parts inside your ears vibrate. Then you hear sound.

▶ **DRAW CONCLUSIONS** How does the sound of a drum reach your ears?

Lesson Wrap-Up

❶ **Vocabulary** What is **sound**?

❷ **Reading Skill** How do you think a guitar string makes a sound?

❸ **Observe** If you see something vibrate, what will you hear?

🔦 **Technology** Visit **www.eduplace.com/scp/** to find out more about sound.

STANDARDS
SC.h.3.1.1.1.1. knows that scientists and technologists use a variety of tools (e.g., thermometers, magnifiers, rulers, and scales) to obtain information in more detail and make work easier.

Thump, Thump

A doctor uses a stethoscope to hear sounds inside your body. Part of the stethoscope vibrates when your heart beats. Vibrations go through tubes on the stethoscope to the doctor's ears.

Sharing Ideas

1. **Write About It** Draw a stethoscope. Write about how sound moves in it.

2. **Talk About It** Talk about questions that you can ask doctors about what they hear through stethoscopes.

How Are Sounds Different?

Science and You

Sometimes people use sounds to make music.

Inquiry Skill

Use Data Compare what you learn to find patterns.

STANDARDS
SC.H.1.1.4.1.1. uses simple graphs, pictures, written statements, and numbers to observe, describe, record, and compare data.

What You Need

5 jars

water

pencil

paper

Different Sounds

Steps

1 Pour different amounts of water into four jars. Leave one jar empty.

2 **Observe** Tap the side of each jar with a pencil. Listen to the sounds.

3 **Record Data** Write letters to order the jars from the lowest sound to the highest sounds.

STEP 1

STEP 2

STEP 3

Think and Share

1. **Use Data** Which jar made the lowest sound? Which made the highest sound? How much water was in those jars?

2. **Infer** How does the amount of water affect the sound?

Investigate More!

Be an Inventor Hum a song. Use the jars to play the song. Add more jars and water if you need them. Then have a class concert.

Vocabulary FCAT

pitch
volume

Reading Skill
Compare and Contrast

STANDARDS
SC.C.2.1.2.1.1. knows that vibrations of objects (for example, strings, drumheads, rubber bands) cause sounds.
SC.B.1.1.4.1.1. knows ways that human activities require and release energy.

Pitch and Volume

Not all sounds are the same. **Pitch** is how high or low a sound is. The faster something vibrates, the higher the sound it makes. Fast vibrations cause a high pitch. Slow vibrations cause a low pitch.

violin with high pitch ▼

bass with low pitch ▶

Volume is how loud or soft a sound is. Think about the sounds you make. When you whisper, you use a little energy to make a soft sound. When you yell, you use a lot of energy to make a loud sound.

loud volume ▲

▶ **COMPARE AND CONTRAST**
How is a high pitch different from a low pitch?

▼ **soft volume**

▲ Smoke alarms beep when something is burning.

Sounds Keep You Safe

Some sounds are warnings that keep you safe. They warn you to get out of the way or to go to a safe place.

Sirens warn drivers to get out of the way.

Lesson Wrap-Up

❶ **Vocabulary** What is **volume**?

❷ **Reading Skill** Compare loud and soft sounds.

❸ **Use Data** What does how fast or slow something vibrates tell about pitch?

🖥 **Technology** Visit **www.eduplace.com/scp/** to find out more about sound.

LINKS for Home and School

Math Find a Sound

Work with four classmates. Give each classmate a bell. Put on a blindfold. Look at the picture to see how to stand.

When one classmate rings a bell, use the words **left**, **right**, **front**, or **back** to tell where you heard the sound.

Music Change the Volume

How do you make the volume of music softer? Play one instrument. Then try to make a softer sound. Play another instrument. Again, try to make a softer sound. Tell what you did each time to make the volume softer.

Visual Summary

Energy sources give off heat, light, or sound.

Heat	Light	Sound
Energy that makes things warm	Energy that you can see	Energy that you can hear

Main Ideas

1. What are three things that give off heat? (pp. F8–F9)

2. Tell one way that energy causes change. (p. F10)

3. How are pitch and volume different? (pp. F26–F27)

4. What are two things that make sounds to keep you safe? (p. F28)

Vocabulary and Science Skills

Choose the correct answer.

5. Heat is a kind of _____.

○ change   ○ energy   ○ shade

6. Which forms when an object blocks light?

○ sunshine   ○ energy   ○ shadow

7. Sound is made when something _____.

○ is still   ○ listens   ○ vibrates

8. Which tells how loud or soft a sound is?

○ pitch   ○ volume   ○ noise

9. Which blocks all light?

○ water   ○ wax paper   ○ a dog

10. Which warms Earth's air, water, and land?

○ a fire   ○ a stove   ○ the Sun

Chapter 13

Moving Faster and Slower

force

push

pull

gravity

machine

speed

motion

force

A push or a pull is a force.

gravity

Gravity is a force that pulls objects toward Earth's center.

speed

Speed is how fast or slow something moves.

motion

Motion is moving from one place to another.

What Makes Things Move?

Science and You

Simple machines can help you move heavy objects.

Inquiry Skill

Communicate Talk to others about what you observe and do.

STANDARDS
SC.H.1.1.3.1.1. works with others to complete an experiment or to solve a problem.

What You Need

objects

paper and pencil

How Things Move

Steps

1 Think of ways to make objects move. You might use one object to move another. See if you can make some things move in a curve.

2 **Record Data** Write how you moved each object.

3 **Communicate** Talk to others about what you observed.

Think and Share

1. What made each object move?

2. **Communicate** Talk about which objects were easier to move.

Investigate More!

Solve a Problem Some children want to play marbles. They need a flat surface. How can they use a marble to find the best place to play?

Vocabulary FCAT

force

push

pull

gravity

machine

Reading Skill

Cause and Effect

STANDARDS
SC.C.2.1.1.1.1. understands various ways gravity affects the motion of objects (for example, an object on a ramp, an object that is dropped).

Pushes and Pulls

A push or a pull is a **force**. A force can make an object change its speed or direction. A **push** is a force that moves something away from you. A **pull** is a force that moves something closer to you.

pull

push

Gravity is a force that pulls objects toward Earth's center. Objects fall to the ground when you drop them because gravity pulls them. Gravity makes you fall down when you trip.

▶ **CAUSE AND EFFECT** What kind of force causes something to move away from you?

Machines That Help

A **machine** is a tool that makes some things easier to do. Ramps, levers, and pulleys are three kinds of machines. People use these machines to move things.

A hammer and a flip top are kinds of levers.

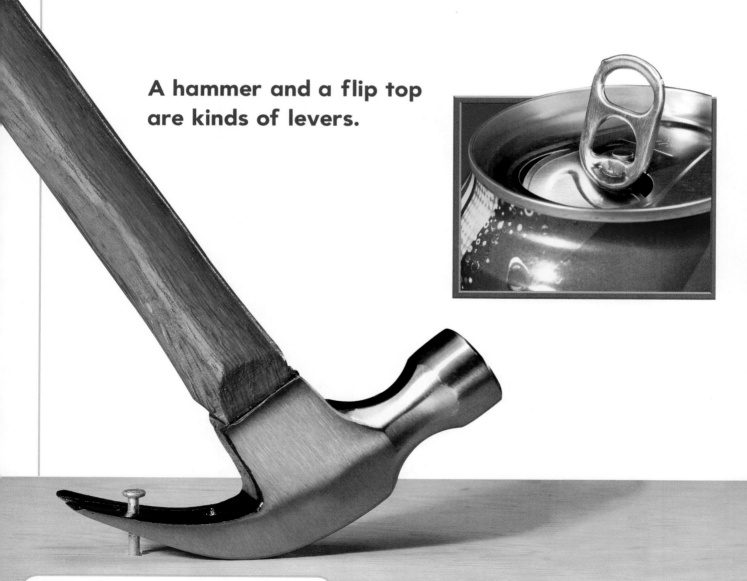

◀ **A pulley makes lifting or moving objects easier.**

A ramp makes it easier to roll things up or down. ▼

▶ **CAUSE AND EFFECT** Why do people use machines?

Lesson Wrap-Up

❶ **Vocabulary** What are two kinds of **force**?

❷ **Reading Skill** What causes objects to move?

❸ **Communicate** How would you explain to a friend what a machine does?

📠 **Technology** Visit **www.eduplace.com/scp/** to find out more about forces.

What Things Move Fast and Slow?

Science and You

You probably move fast when you go down a hill and slow when you go up.

Inquiry Skill

Compare You can look for ways that objects move at different speeds.

STANDARDS
SC.C.2.1.1.1.1. understands various ways gravity affects the motion of objects (for example, an object on a ramp, an object that is dropped).

What You Need

2 books

cardboard

toy car

tape

Compare Distance

Steps

STEP 1

1. Make a ramp by placing cardboard on the edge of one book.

2. Let a car go from the top of the ramp. Put a piece of tape where the car stops.

STEP 2

3. **Experiment** Stack two books. Make a new ramp by placing cardboard at the edge of the top book. Repeat Step 2.

STEP 3

Think and Share

1. **Compare** Which time did the car travel farther?

2. **Infer** Why did the car travel farther that time?

Investigate More!

Experiment Take the car apart. Try each part on a ramp. Compare the distance each part travels with the distance the car traveled in Step 2.

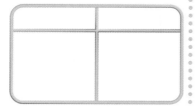
Speed

Speed is how fast or slow something moves. Some things move at a fast speed. An airplane flies fast. Juice can be poured fast. Some objects move at a slow speed. A caterpillar moves slowly. Honey drips slowly.

▶ **CLASSIFY** Name two things that move fast.

◀ fast

◀ slow

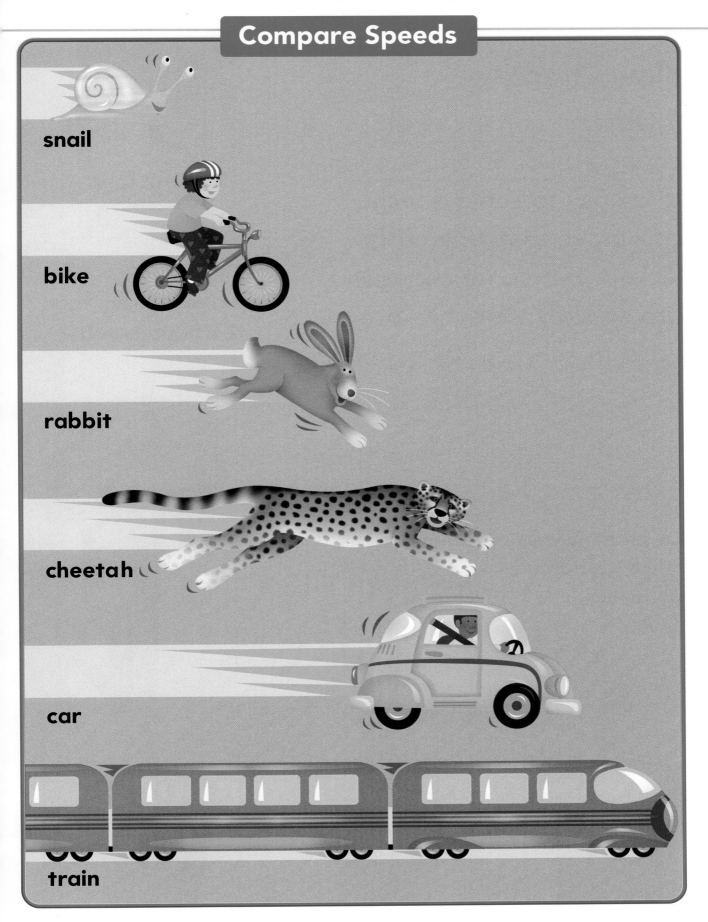

snail

bike

rabbit

cheetah

car

train

▲ **Different things move at different speeds.**

Slow Changes

Objects can move or change at different speeds. It is easy to see a soccer ball move fast when it is kicked. But some changes are so slow that they are hard to see.

The minute hand moves faster than the hour hand.

A plant grows so slowly that you cannot see it moving.

You cannot see plants and people grow while you watch. You can tell that they have grown if you measure them at different times.

▶ **CLASSIFY** What are some things that change slowly?

People grow slowly. ▶

Lesson Wrap-Up

❶ **Vocabulary** What tells how fast or slowly an object moves?

❷ **Reading Skill** Describe the speeds of a snail moving and a flower blooming.

❸ **Compare** Which moves at a faster speed, a rabbit or a train?

Technology Visit **www.eduplace.com/scp/** to find out more about speed.

A Wild Ride

Cast
Ms. Taylor, Maria, Jane, Ray, and Alex

Ms. Taylor: Today is show-and-tell day. Who has something to share?

Maria, Jane, Ray, Alex: We do!

Jane: We all went to Walt Disney World Resort.

Ms. Taylor: What rides did you like?

Ray: Anything that went really fast.

Maria: I like *Space Mountain*. The roller coaster goes up the hill slowly.

STANDARDS
SC.C.1.1.1.1.1. knows the relative order of speeds of various objects (for example, snails, turtles, tricycles, bicycles, cars, jets, rockets).

READING LINK

Ray: And when it goes down, it goes faster and faster!

Alex: I'm glad roller coasters have brakes to slow down!

Jane: I like *Splash Mountain*. You go down fast. When you splash in the water, you slow down.

Alex: I like *It's a Small World*. Your boat goes slow so you can see all the different children.

Ms. Taylor: It sounds as if Walt Disney World Resort is fun at any speed.

Sharing Ideas

1. **Write About It** Tell about a ride you like. Does it go fast or slow?

2. **Talk About It** Why do you think you need to be a certain height to ride on some roller coasters?

What Makes Things Speed Up or Slow Down?

Science and You

You can use forces to make objects go faster or slower.

Inquiry Skill

Measure You can use a tool to find how much or how many.

tape

toy car

paper-clip chain

STANDARDS
SC.H.1.1.5.1.2. uses standard (for example, centimeters) and nonstandard units (for example, paper clips, hands, pencils) to measure organisms and objects and parts of organisms and objects.

Change Motion

Steps

1. Use tape to mark a starting place. Place a car at the tape mark. Gently roll the car. Use tape to mark where the car stops.

STEP 1

2. **Measure** Use a paper-clip chain to measure how far the car went. Record your data.

STEP 2

3. Start again at the first tape mark. Try to roll the car farther than you did the first time. Repeat step 2.

STEP 3

Think and Share

1. **Compare** What did you do to change how far the car went?

2. **Infer** How does force change how objects

Investigate More!

Ask Questions What else can you do to change how the car moves? Finish the question: What would happen if I _____?

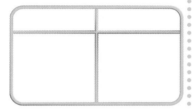

STANDARDS
SC.C.1.1.2.1.1. knows that various things move at different speeds when different forces are applied.

Motion

Motion is moving from one place to another. You can use force to change the motion of something. You can use a lot of force or a little force. You can stop motion, too.

▶ **COMPARE AND CONTRAST** How can you change motion?

The kicker changes the direction of the ball when she kicks it. The harder she kicks, the farther the ball goes.

Catching the ball stops its motion.

The player pushes the ball when he rolls it. The harder he rolls it, the faster the ball moves.

Moving Heavy Objects

Heavy objects are harder to move than light objects. You have to use more force to move a heavy object. Heavy objects are harder to stop, too.

heavy

light
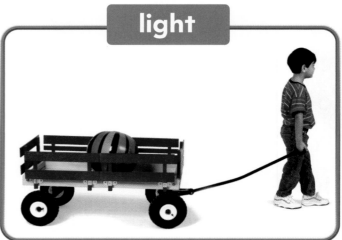

Lesson Wrap-Up

❶ **Vocabulary** What is **motion**?

❷ **Reading Skill** Compare moving a heavy book with moving a light book.

❸ **Measure** How many hands fit across your desk?

💻 **Technology** Visit **www.eduplace.com/scp/** to find out more about motion.

LINKS
for Home and School

Math Direction and Position

Make word cards using the words below. First, pick a card. Then have a partner act out the word on the card. Say what your partner is doing.

to the left	**under**
to the right	**above**
away from	**inside**
toward	**outside**

You are walking toward the door.

toward

Social Studies Around Town

Draw a picture to show ways that people move from one place to another in your town.

Visual Summary

Forces can change the speed and motion of things.

Forces			Speed		Motion	
Push	Pull	Gravity	Fast	Slow	Start	Stop

Main Ideas

1. What makes objects change speed or direction? (p. F36)

2. Name two machines and tell what they do. (pp. F38–F39)

3. Sometimes you cannot see something change. Tell why. (p. F44)

4. How can you change motion? (pp. F50–F51)

Vocabulary and Science Skills

Choose the correct answer.

5. Gravity is a force that _____.

○ lifts   ○ pulls   ○ pushes

6. Which tells how fast something is moving?

○ gravity   ○ motion   ○ speed

7. Tools that make things easier to do are _____.

○ forces   ○ machines   ○ gravity

8. A push or a pull is a _____.

○ force   ○ motion   ○ object

9. Which can move fastest?

○ train   ○ car   ○ rabbit

10. Which changes the motion of something?

○ force   ○ speed   ○ direction

Discover!

What is the fastest a human can run?

At the Olympics in 1996, a man ran 200 meters in 19.32 seconds. That's about 23 miles an hour. But compared to a cheetah, humans are slow. A cheetah can run three times as fast!

Go to **www.eduplace.com/scp/** to see animals and objects that move fast and slow.

Science and Math Toolbox

Using a Hand Lens. H2

Using a Thermometer. H3

Using a Ruler H4

Using a Calculator H5

Using a Balance H6

Making a Chart H7

Making a Tally Chart H8

Making a Bar Graph H9

Using a Hand Lens

A hand lens is a tool that makes objects look bigger. It helps you see the small parts of an object.

Look at a Coin

1. Place a coin on your desk.

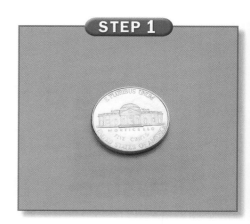

STEP 1

2. Hold the hand lens above the coin. Look through the lens. Slowly move the lens away from the coin. What do you see?

3. Keep moving the lens away until the coin looks blurry.

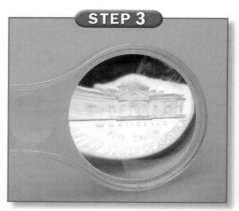

STEP 3

4. Then slowly move the lens closer. Stop when the coin does not look blurry.

STEP 4

Using a Thermometer

A thermometer is a tool used to measure temperature. Temperature tells how hot or cold something is. It is measured in degrees.

Find the Temperature of Water

1 Put water into a cup.

2 Put a thermometer into the cup.

3 Watch the colored liquid in the thermometer. What do you see?

4 Look how high the colored liquid is. What number is closest? That is the temperature of the water.

Using a Ruler

A ruler is a tool used to measure the length of objects. Rulers measure length in inches or centimeters.

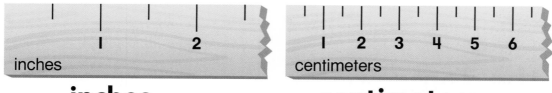

inches　　　　　**centimeters**

Measure a Crayon

1. Place the ruler on your desk.

2. Lay your crayon next to the ruler. Line up one end with the end of the ruler.

3. Look at the other end of the crayon. Which number is closest to that end?

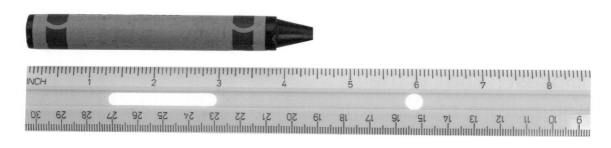

Using a Calculator

A calculator is a tool that can help you add and subtract numbers.

Subtract Numbers

1 Tim and Anna grew plants. Tim grew 5 plants. Anna grew 8 plants.

2 How many more plants did Anna grow? Use your calculator to find out.

3 Enter **8** on the calculator. Then press the **−** key. Enter **5** and press **=** .

What is your answer?

Tim's Plants

Anna's Plants

Using a Balance

A balance is a tool used to measure mass. Mass is the amount of matter in an object.

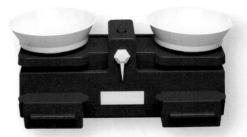

Compare the Mass of Objects

1. Check that the pointer is on the middle mark of the balance. If needed, move the slider on the back to the left or right.

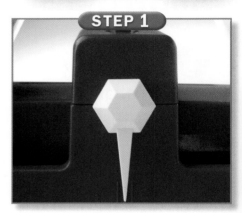

STEP 1

2. Place a clay ball in one pan. Place a crayon in the other pan.

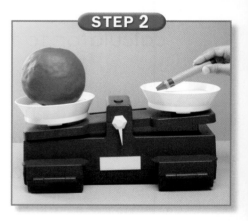

STEP 2

3. Observe the positions of the two pans.

Does the clay ball or the crayon have more mass?

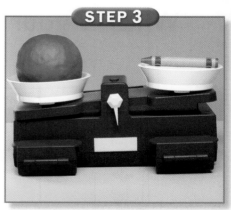

STEP 3

Making a Chart

A chart can help you sort information, or data. When you sort data it is easier to read and compare.

Make a Chart to Compare Animals

1 Give the chart a title.

2 Name the groups that tell about the data you collect. Label the columns with the names.

3 Carefully fill in the data in each column.

Which animal can move in the most ways?

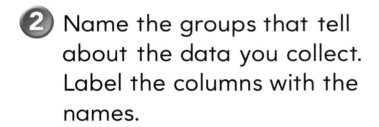

How Animals Move	
Animal	How It Moves
fish	swim
dog	walk, swim
duck	walk, fly, swim

Making a Tally Chart

A tally chart helps you keep track of items as you count.

Make a Tally Chart of Kinds of Pets

Jan's class made a tally chart to record the number of each kind of pet they own.

1 Every time they counted one pet, they made one tally.

2 When they got to five, they made the fifth tally a line across the other four.

3 Count the tallies to find each total.

How many of each kind of pet do the children have?

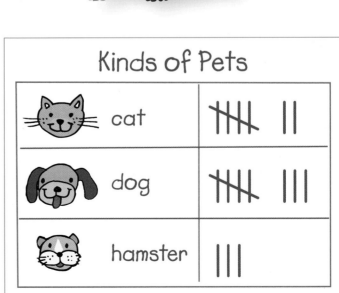

Kinds of Pets

🐱	cat	卌 ||
🐶	dog	卌 |||
🐹	hamster	|||

Making a Bar Graph

A bar graph can help you sort and compare data.

Make a Bar Graph of Favorite Pets

You can use the data in the tally chart on page H8 to make a bar graph.

1. Choose a title for your graph.

2. Write numbers along the side.

3. Write pet names along the bottom.

4. Start at the bottom of each column. Fill in one box for each tally.

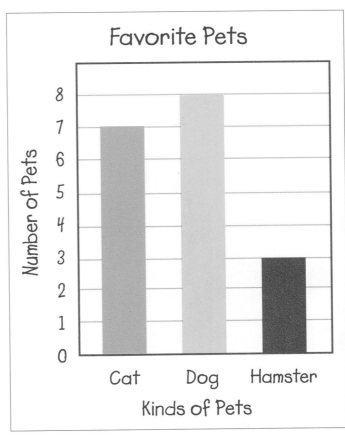

Which pet is the favorite?

Health and Fitness Handbook

Are you healthy? You are if you:

- know how your body works.
- practice safe actions when you play.
- know how to stay well.
- are active every day.
- eat healthful foods.

Inside Your Body..............................H12
Learn some of the body parts that
let you run, think, and breathe.

**Foods for Healthy Bones
and Teeth**...H14
Find out which foods help keep
bones and teeth strong.

Caring for Your Teeth.......................H15
Brush and floss for healthy teeth.

Fun and Fit on the Playground......H16
Find out how to make your body
stronger as you play.

A Safe Bike H17
Are you safe on your bike?
Find out.

Inside Your Body

Your body has many parts. All the parts work together.

Brain

Your brain helps you think. It controls all your other body parts.

Lungs

Air goes in and out of your lungs. Your body needs air to stay alive.

Heart

Your heart pumps blood through your body. Your heart is about the size of your fist.

Stomach

Your stomach helps change food so your body can use it.

Bones and muscles hold you up and help you move.

Bones

Your body has more than 200 bones. Some bones protect body parts.

- Your skull protects your brain.
- Your ribs protect your heart and lungs.
- There are 27 bones in each of your hands.

Muscles

Muscles move body parts.

- The muscles in your legs are large. They help you run, jump, and play.
- The muscles in your eyelids are tiny. They help you blink.
- Your heart is a muscle, too.

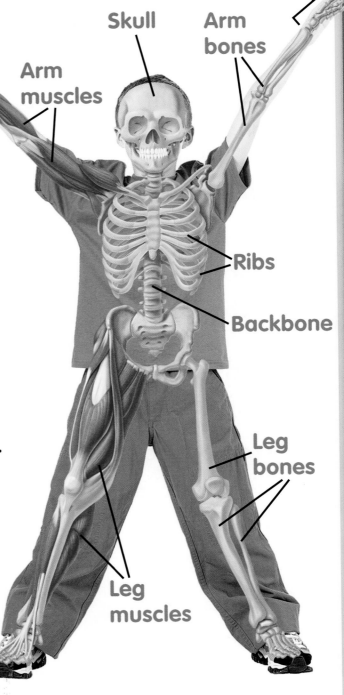

Hand bones

Skull

Arm bones

Arm muscles

Ribs

Backbone

Leg bones

Leg muscles

Foods for Healthy Bones and Teeth

Your body needs calcium. Calcium makes bones and teeth strong. Get the right amount of calcium by eating three of these foods every day!

Dairy Foods

- milk
- yogurt
- cheese

Foods With Calcium Added

- cereal bars
- wheat bread
- cereal
- juices
- tofu
- waffles

Other Foods

- spinach
- bok choy
- garbanzo beans
- almonds

These foods give you one serving of calcium.

calcium-added orange juice

breakfast bar

two burritos

macaroni and cheese

Caring for Your Teeth

You use your teeth to chew, talk, and smile.

Brush Twice Each Day

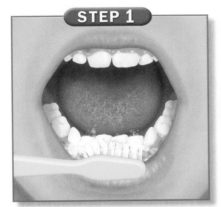
STEP 1
Brush the fronts.

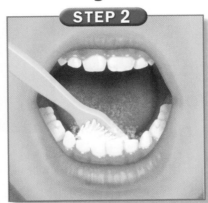
STEP 2
Brush the backs.

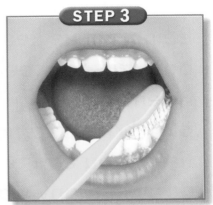
STEP 3
Brush the tops.

Floss Once Each Day

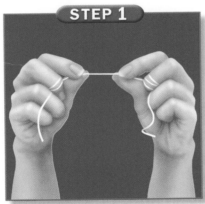
STEP 1
Wrap the floss and pull it tight.

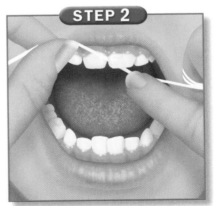
STEP 2
Slide the floss between teeth.

Dental Check-Ups

Dentists and dental hygienists clean and check your teeth. They use x-ray machines to check the hidden parts of teeth.

Fun and Fit on the Playground

Have Some Fun

It's time to go outside. How will you play today? Being active keeps your body fit. You feel good when you are fit. You can play hard and not get tired. You can bend your body in many ways.

Throw, kick, and catch.

Getting and Staying Fit

Do different activities to get fit and stay fit. Stretch before you start. Play hard. Then stretch again. Try these Fun and Fit ideas.

Climb, skip, or swing.

Have fun with friends.

A Safe Bike

You probably know how to ride a bike. Is your bike the right size? Your feet should reach the pedals easily. Your body should be above the bar when you stand.

Safety Equipment

Wear a helmet every time you ride. It should fit flat and protect your forehead. Pull the strap tight.

The right equipment can help keep you safe.

bell

front reflector

rear reflector

reflector

pedal reflectors

Picture Glossary

 A

adult
A full-grown plant, animal, or person. (A46)

air pollution
Harmful things that get into the air. (C36)

amphibian
An animal that has wet skin with no hair, feathers, or scales. (A42)

attracts
Pulls toward. A magnet attracts iron and steel. (E20)

 B

boulders
Very large rocks. (C15)

C

classify

Sort objects into groups that are alike in some way.

cloud

Many drops of water together. (D23)

communicate

Share what you learn with others by talking, drawing pictures, or making charts and graphs.

compare

Look for ways that objects or events are alike or different.

cone

The part of a pine tree where seeds grow. (A22)

D

desert

A place with very little water. (B42)

dissolve

To mix completely in water. (E52)

E

energy

Something that can cause change or do work. Heat is energy. (F8)

evaporate

To change from a liquid to a gas. (E46)

exercise

Movement that keeps your body strong. (A67)

experiment

Make a plan to collect data and then share the results with others.

F

fall

The season that follows summer. In fall, the weather gets cooler. (D34)

fins

Body parts that help a fish move. (A34)

float

To stay on top of water. (E28)

flowers

The parts of plants that make seeds. (A11)

food

What living things use to get energy. (B16)

force

A push or a pull. A force can move an object. (F36)

forest

A place with many trees that grow close together. (B28)

freeze

To change from a liquid to a solid. A pond may freeze in winter. (E44)

gas

Matter that changes shape to fill all the space it is in. (E41)

gills

Parts of a fish that help it breathe under water. (A41)

gravity

A force that pulls objects toward Earth's center. Gravity pulls you down a slide. (F37)

heat

A kind of energy that makes things warm. (F8)

humus

Bits of rotting plants and animals in soil. (C24)

I

infant

A new baby. (A64)

infer

Use what you observe and know to tell what you think.

L

leaves

Parts of a plant that make food for the plant. (A10)

life cycle

The order of changes that happen in the lifetime of a plant or animal. (A22)

light

A kind of energy that you can see. (F14)

liquid

Matter that flows and takes the shape of its container. (E40)

living thing

Something that grows, changes, and makes other living things like itself. (B8)

lungs

Body parts that take in air. Birds and mammals use lungs to breathe. (A40)

machine

A tool that makes some things easier to do. A pulley is a machine. (F38)

magnet

An object that pulls iron and steel toward it. (E20)

magnify

To make something look larger. (E14)

mammal

An animal whose mother makes milk to feed her babies. (A40)

matter

What all things are made of. (E8)

measure

Use different tools to collect data about the properties of objects.

melt

To change from a solid to a liquid. Ice on a frozen pond will melt in spring. (E44)

mineral

A nonliving thing found in nature. A rock is made of one or more minerals. (C14)

mixture

Two or more kinds of matter put together. A sandwich is a mixture. (E50)

Moon

A space object close to Earth. (D58)

motion

Moving from one place to another. (F50)

natural resource

Something from Earth that people use. Water is a natural resource. (C8)

nonliving thing

Something that does not eat, drink, grow, and make other things like itself. (B10)

O

observe

Use tools and the senses to learn about the properties of an object or event.

ocean

A large body of salty water. (B34)

pitch

How high or low a sound is.
A violin has a high pitch. (F26)

planet

A space object that moves
around the Sun. (D48)

predict

Use what you know and patterns
you observe to tell what will
happen.

property

Anything that you learn about an
object by using your senses. (E10)

pull

A force that moves something
closer to you. (F36)

push

A force that moves something
away from you. (F36)

R

record data

Write or draw to show what you have observed.

recycle

To take an object and make a new object from it. (C50)

reduce

To use less of something. (C52)

repel

To push away. Like poles of magnets repel each other. (E22)

reptile

An animal that has dry skin with scales. (A42)

reuse

To use something again. Watts Towers reuse tiles, seashells, and glass. (C48)

roots

The parts of a plant that take in water from the ground. (A9)

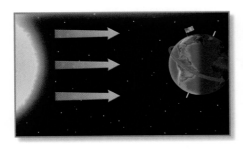

rotates

Spins. Day and night happen when Earth rotates. (D52)

S

season

A time of year that has its own kind of weather. (D28)

seed

The part of a plant that has a new plant inside it. (A11)

seedling

A young plant. (A22)

senses

Sight, smell, hearing, touch, and taste. You can see, smell, hear, feel, and taste popcorn. (A56)

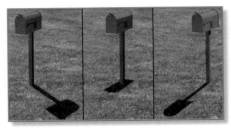

shadow

Something that forms when an object blocks light. (D68, F17)

shelter

A safe place for animals to live. (B20)

sink

To drop to the bottom of water. (E28)

sleep

Rest for body and mind. (A68)

soil

The loose top layer of Earth. (C24)

solid

Matter that has its own shape. (E38)

sound

A kind of energy that you can hear. Birds make sounds when they sing. (F20)

speed

How fast or slow something moves. Juice pours at a faster speed than honey. (F42)

spines

Sharp points on a cactus. (A14)

spring

The season that follows winter. Many baby animals are born in spring. (D28)

star

A space object that makes its own light. (D48)

stem

Part of a plant that connects the roots to the other plant parts. (A9)

summer

The season that follows spring. Summer is the warmest season. (D30)

Sun

The brightest space object in the day sky. (D47)

sunlight

Energy from the Sun. (B16)

teen

A person between 13 and 19 years old. (A65)

temperature

How warm or cool something is. The temperature is cold when there is snow. (D14)

thermometer

A tool that measures temperature. (D14)

use data

Use what you observe and record to find patterns and make predictions.

Measurements of My Plants	
Date	Measurement
October 1	3 inches
November 1	4 inches
December 1	$4\frac{1}{2}$ inches
January 1	5 inches
February 1	6 inches

use models

Use something like the real thing to understand how the real thing works.

use numbers

Count, measure, order, or estimate to descibe and compare objects and events.

vibrates

Moves back and forth very fast. A drum vibrates when you strike it. (F20)

volume

How loud or soft a sound is. A whisper has soft volume. (F27)

water cycle

Water moving from Earth to the sky and back again. (D22)

water pollution

Harmful things that get into water. (C42)

weather

What the air outside is like. (D8)

weigh

To find out how heavy an object is. (E16)

wetland

A low area of land that is very wet. (B36)

wings

Body parts that help a bird fly through the air. (A34)

winter

The season that follows fall. Winter is the coldest season. (D36)

work together

Work as a group to share ideas, data, and observations.

Index

Adult, A29, A46, A65
Air
    in deserts, B42, B43
    floating and, E29, E56
    as a gas, E41
    heating of, F8
    light and, F16
    as natural resource, C8,
      C10, C11, C34–C37
    need of living things,
      B8, B13, B19
    pollution of, C31,
      C36–C37
    in soil, C24–C25
    sound and, F21–F22
Amphibian, A42
Animals, A28
    adult, A29, A46–A47
    air and, C34
    amphibians, A42
    birds, A34, A41, D29,
      F21
    body parts, A32–A35,
      A43, A58
    of deserts, B42–B44
    fish, A41
    food for, A17, A43,
      B16–B17, D31
    of forests, B28–B31
    life cycle, A46–A48
    mammal, A29, A40
    needs of, A10, B13,
      B16–B20, C11
    of oceans, B34–B35
    pollution and, C42
    reptiles, A29, A42
    seasons and, D29, D31,
      D35, D37
    soil and, C25
    of wetlands, B36–B37
Attract, E20–E25

Balance, E16
Biography
    Douglas, Marjory
      Stoneman, B38–B39
    Galilei, Galileo,
      D62–D63
Birds
    body parts, A34–A35,
      A41
    food for, A17
    hummingbird, A72
    spring and, D29
    wings of, A34–A35, A41
Boulders, C15

Cactus, A14, B44
Careers
    astronaut, D58,
      D62–D63
    environmentalist,
      B38–B39
    scientist, D62–D63
    writer, B38–B39
Cloud, D5, D23, D24–D25
Cone, A5, A22–A23

Day, D46–D47, D52–D53
Daylight, D28, D30, D34,
    D36
Desert, B25, B42–B44
Dissolve, E52
Douglas, Marjory
    Stoneman, B38–B39

Earth
    air, C8, C10, C11
    land, C8, C10–C11
    light from the Sun, F14
    Moon and, D60
    natural resources,
      C8–C11, C14–C17
    as a planet, D48
    rotation of, D52–D55,
      D67
    soil, C2, C24–C26
    Sun and, D47, F8
    water, C8–C9
Energy
    causes change, F10–F11
    from food, A66
    heat, F5, F8–F11
    light, F5, F14–F17
    sleep and, A68
    sound, F5, F20–F22,
      F27
Evaporate, E46
Exercise, A53, A60–A61,
    A66–A67

Fall, D34–D35, D38, E45
Fins, A29, A34, B35
Fire, B11
    heat from, F9–F11
    light from, F14
    water and, C41
Fish, A34, A41, B34–B35
Float, E28–E30, E56
Florida,
    activity trails in,
      A60–A61
    cold weather in, E47
    Everglades, B38–B39
    safety at the beaches
      of, C44–C45

space exploration and, D62–D63

Flower, A8, A11, A14, A18–A19

Food
of animals, A17, A43, D31
need of living things, B5, B13, B16–B17
of people, A16, A66, A69

Food chain, B17

Force, F33, F36–F39, F50–F52

Forest, B25, B28–B31

Freeze, E44–E45

Galilei, Galileo, D62–D63

Gas, E35, E41, E46

Gills, A41, B35

Gravity, F33, F37

Hand lens, E14–E15

Health and Safety
Florida Activity Trails, A60–A61
Safety at the Beach, C44–C45

Hearing, A56–A57, E8–E11, F22

Heat, F5, F8–F11

Humus, C5, C24

Ichetucknee Springs State Park, A60

Infant, A53, A64

Inquiry Skills
ask questions, A7, A31, A45, B15, B33, D21, F12, F13, F49
be an inventor, D13, F25
classify, A13, A38, A39, B6, B7, B33, C7, C13, C46, C47, D32, D33, E6, E7, F13
communicate, A39, A45, A54, A55, A63, B26, B27, C13, C39, D26, D27, D33, E7, E37, E43, E49, F34, F35
compare, A12, A13, A31, A45, A63, B7, B32, B33, B41, C13, C47, D20, D21, D33, D45, E13, E19, E36, E37, F7, F19, F40, F41, F49
experiment, A21, A55, B41, C12, C13, C23, C33, C39, D27, D51, D57, D65, E19, E27, E43, F7, F41
infer, A30, A31, A63, B15, B27, B41, C7, C23, C33, C39, C47, D21, D27, D50, D51, E18, E19, E27, E43, F7, F19, F25, F41, F49
measure, D12, D13, D21, E12, E13, F6, F7, F48, F49
observe, A6, A7, A21, A31, A45, A63, B7, B14, B15, B27, C13, C22, C23, C33, D7, D21, D44, D45, D65, E13, E19, E27, E37, E43, E48, E49, F13, F18, F19, F25
predict, D21, D27, D51, D64, D65, E19, E26, E27, E42, E43, E49, F13

record data, A7, A13, A39, B7, B27, C33, C47, D6, D7, D13, D45, D65, E7, E19, E27, F7, F13, F19, F25, F35
solve a problem, A39, C47, D33, E13, E37, F19, F35
use data, C7, C32, C33, F24, F25
use models, A20, A21, A44, A45, A55, C38, C39, D51, D56, D57
use numbers, B40, B41, C6, C7, D57
work together, A13, A62, A63, B7, B27, C7, D7, D45, E7, E49

Investigate
cat's life cycle, A44–A45
change motion, F48–F49
classify animals, A38–A39
classify objects, B6–B7, E6–E7
collect pollution, C32–C33
compare animals, B32–B33
compare distance, F40–F41
compare leaves, A12–A13
compare matter, E36–E37
compare rocks, C12–C13
day and night, D50–D51
different sounds, F24–F25
float or sink, E26–E27
grow plants, D26–D27
hidden animals, A30–A31
how things move, F34–F35

land and water, C6–C7
make a mixture,
    E48–E49
make sounds, F18–F19
measure heat, F6–F7
measure weather,
    D12–D13
model your body,
    A54–A55
Moon changes,
    D56–D57
observe a plant, A6–A7
observe plants,
    B14–B15
observe sky, D44–D45
observe soil, C22–C23
observe a tree,
    B26–B27
person's life, A62–A63
predict changes,
    E42–E43
record weather, D6–D7
shine light, F12–F13
sort your trash,
    C46–C47
Sun changes, D64–D65
use magnets, E18–E19
use plant models,
    A20–A21
use tools, E12–E13
water changes,
    D20–D21
waterwheel, C38–C39
wet or dry, B40–B41
what to wear,
    D32–D33

Leaves, A8, A10, A14,
    A18–A19, D34
Levers, F38
Life cycle
    of animals, A46–A47,
        D29
    of people, A64–A65
    of plants, A22–A23

Light
    in day, D46
    energy of, F5, F14–F17
    stars and, D48
**Links for Home and
School**
    art, E53
    language arts, A49,
        B45, D69, E31
    math, A25, A49, A69,
        B21, B45, C27, C53,
        D39, D69, E31, E53,
        F29, F53
    music, A25, C27, F29
    social studies, A69, B21,
        C53, D39, F53
Liquid, E35, E40, E52
    adding solids to, E52
    change to gas, E46
    change to solid,
        E44–E45
Literature
    Animal Disguises, A37
    "City Rain," D19
    "Ice Cycle," E47
    "In a Winter Meadow,"
        A36
    Rain, D18
Living things, B5
    of deserts, B42–B44
    of forests, B28–B31
    needs of, B8–B9,
        B16–B20
    nonliving things or,
        B12–B13
    of oceans, B34–B35
    of wetlands, B36–B37
Lungs, A40–A41

Machine, F38–F39
Magnet, E5, E20–E23,
    E51
Magnify, E5, E14–E15

Mammal, A29, A40
Matter, E5
    change in form,
        E44–E46
    floating and sinking,
        E28–E30
    forms of, E38–E41
    length of, E17
    magnets and, E20–E23
    magnified, E14–E15
    mixtures of, E50–E52
    properties of, E10–E11,
        E16, E20–E23,
        E28–E30
    senses and, E8–E11
    weight of, E16, E29
Measuring tapes, E17
Melt, E35, E44–E45
Mineral, C5, C14–C17,
    C56
Mixture, E50–E52
Moon, D43, D48,
    D58–D61, D63, D67
Motion, F33, F36–F39,
    F50–F52

Natural resource, C5
    air, C8, C10, C11,
        C34–C37
    land, C8, C10
    reuse, recycle, reduce,
        C48–C52
    rocks and minerals,
        C14–C17
    soil, C24–C27
    water, C8–C9, C40–C43
Night, D48, D54–D55
Nonliving thing, B5,
    B10–B11
    of deserts, B42–B43
    of forests, B28–B29
    living things or, B12–B13
    of oceans, B34–B35

Ocean, B25, B34–B35, C9, C40, C41
Oxygen, A10

Patterns, A25
day and night, D52–D55
seasons, D28–D31, D34–D38
water cycle, D22–D23
People, A52
air and, C34–C35
body parts, A56–A59
changes, F45
exercise and, A60–A61, A66–A67
food for, A16, B17
growing and changing, A64–A65
living things, B8–B10
needs of, A66–A69
pollution and, C36–C37, C42–C43
senses of, A56–A57
use of land, C10
use of rocks, C16–C17
use of water, C8, C40–C41
Pitch, F26
Planet, D43, D48
Plants, A4
air and, C34, C37
of deserts, B44
eating, A16–A17, D31
in forests, B28–B31
growth, F45
life cycle of, A22–A23
needs of, B8, B16–B19, C24–C25

parts of, A8–A11
pollution and, C42
seasons and, D28–D29, D31, D37
sorting, A14–A15
sunlight and, B16
uses for, A18–A19
of wetlands, B36–B37
Property
floating and sinking, E28–E30
length, E17
magnets and, E21
senses and, E10–E11
weight, E16
Pull, F36
Pulleys, F38–F39
Push, F36

Rain
clouds and, D11, D23–D25
measuring, D16–D17
plants and, D28
Rain gauge, D16–D17
Ramps, F38–F39
Readers' Theater
Fast Rides and Slow Lines, F46–47
Living or Nonliving, B12–B13
Rock Stars, C18–C19
Reading in Science
Dirt, C2–C3
Energy: Heat, Light, and Fuel, F2–F3
Over in the Meadow, B2–B3
What Is the World Made Of?, E2–E3
What's Alive?, A2–A3
What Will the Weather Be?, D2–D3

Recycle, C31, C48, C50–C51
Reduce, C48, C52
Repel, E22–E23
Reptile, A29, A42
Reuse, C31, C48–C49
Rocks, C10, C14–C17, C18–C21, C56
Roots, A5, A8–A9, A14, A18–A19
Rotates, D52–D55
Ruler, E17

Salamanders, A42, A46–A47
Science inquiry, S6
Season, D5
fall, D34–D35, D38
pattern of, D38
spring, D28–D29, D38
summer, D30–D31, D38
winter, D36–D38
Seed, A5, A11, A14, A18–A19, A22–A23
Seedlings, A22–A23
Senses, A53, A56–A57, E8–E11
Shadow, D68, D69, F17
Shape
floating and sinking and, E29–E30
gases, E41
liquids, E40
solids, E39
Shells, B48
Shelter, B5, B20
Sight, A56–A57, E8–E11
Sink, E5, E28–E30, E56
Sky
in day, D46–D47, D52–D53
at night, D48–D49, D54–D55

Sleep, A68
Sleet, D23
Smell, A56–A57, E8–E11
Snow, D25, D36–D37
Soil, C2, C5, C24–C26
Solid, E35, E38–E39
  in liquids, E52
  melting, E35, E44–E45
  mixtures of, E50–E52
Sound
  as energy, F5, F20–F22
  pitch, F26
  and safety, F28
  vibrations, F20–F22,
    F26
  volume, F5, F27
Space, B13, B18–B19
Speed, F33, F42–F45, F56
Spines, A5, A14
Spring, D28–D29, D38,
  E45
Star, D43, D47, D48, D67
Stem, A8, A9, A18–A19
Summer, D30–D31, D38
Sun, D43
  day and, D47, D52–D53
  Earth and, D66–D68
  heat from, F8, F10
  light from, F14
  Moon and, D59
  night and, D48,
    D54–D55
  shadows and, D68, F17
  water cycle and, D22
Sunlight, B16

Taste, A56–A57, E8–E11
Technology, S11
  Mighty Magnets,
    E24–E25
  Plant Power!, A18–A19
  Thump, Thump!, F23
Teen, A53, A65

Temperature, D14–D15
Thermometer, D5,
  D14–D15
Tools
  balance, E16
  hand lens, E14–E15
  machines, F38–F39
  for measuring weather,
    D14–D17
  rulers and measuring
    tapes, E17
  thermometer, D5,
    D14–D15
Touch, A56–A57, E8–E11
Trees, A14, C10
  forests, B25, B28–B31
  life cycle of, A22–A23
  uses for, A18

Vibrate, F20–F22, F26
Volume, F5, F27

Water, C40–C43
  change to gas, E46
  change to solid,
    E44–E45
  in clouds, D5, D23
  cycle, D22–D23
  deserts and, B25, B42
  fish, A41
  heating of, F8
  as natural resource,
    C8–C9
  need of living things,
    B13, B18–B19
  in oceans, B25, B34, C9
  pollution of, C31,
    C42–C43
  rain, D11, D16,
    D23–D25, D28

  soil and, C24, C25, C26
  in wetlands, B25, B36
Water cycle, D22–D23
Weather, D5
  changes, D10–D11
  clouds and, D24–D25
  in fall, D34–D35
  kinds of, D8–D11
  in spring, D28–D29
  in summer, D30–D31
  tools to measure,
    D14–D17
  in winter, D36–D37
Weigh, E16, E29
Wetland, B25, B36–B37,
  B38–B39
Windsock, D16
Wind vane, D16
Wings, A34–A35, A41
Winter, D36–D38, E45

Credits

Permission Acknowledgements

TRO © Copyright 1956 (Renewed), 1958 (Renewed), 1970 (Renewed), and 1972 (Renewed) Ludlow Music, Inc., New York, N.Y. Used by Permission. Excerpt from The Latest Look from Animal Disguises, by Belinda Weber. Copyright © 2004 Kingfisher Publications Plc. Reprinted by permission of Kingfisher Publications Plc, an imprint of Houghton Mifflin Company. Excerpt from In A Winter Meadow from The Frogs Wore Red Suspenders, by Jack Prelutsky. Copyright © 2002 by Jack Prelutsky. Reprinted by permission of HarperCollins Publishers. Excerpt from What's Alive?, by Kathleen Weidner Zoehfeld, illustrated by Nadine Bernard Westcott. Text copyright © 1995 by Kathleen Weidner Zoehfeld. Illustrations copyright © 1995 by Nadine Bernard Westcott. Reprinted by permission of HarperCollins Publishers. Excerpt from Over in the Meadow, by Ezra Jack Keats. Copyright © 1971 by Ezra Jack Keats. Copyright © renewed 1999 by Martin Pope, Executor of Ezra Jack Keats. Illustrations copyright © assigned to Ezra Jack Keats Foundation. Reprinted by permission of the Ezra Jack Keats Foundation and of Viking Children's Books, a division of Penguin Young Readers Group, a member of Penguin Group (USA) Inc., 345 Hudson Street, New York, NY 10014. All rights reserved. Excerpt from Dirt, by Steve "The Dirtmeister" Tomacek, illustrated by Nancy Woodman. Text copyright © 2002 by Stephen M. Tomacek. Illustrations copyright © 2002 by Nancy Woodman. Reprinted by permission of National Geographic Society. Excerpt from City Rain from Taxis and Toadstools, by Rachel Field. Copyright © 1926 by Doubleday, a division of Random House, Inc. Reprinted by permission of Random House Children's Books, a division of Random House, Inc. Rain, by Manya Stojic. Copyright © 2000 by Manya Stojic. Reprinted by permission of Crown Publishers, an imprint of Random House Children's Books, a division of Random House, Inc. Excerpt from What Will the Weather Be?, illustrated by Carolyn Croll. Text copyright © 1991 by Lynda DeWitt. Illustrations copyright © 1991 by Carolyn Croll. Reprinted by permission of HarperCollins Publishers. Ice Cycle, by Mary Ann Hoberman, from Once Upon Ice and Other Frozen Poems, selected by Jane Yolen, illustrated by Jason Stemple. Text Copyright © 1997 by Mary Ann Hoberman. Photographs copyright © 1997 by Jason Stemple. Text reprinted by permission of Gina Maccoby Literary Agency. Photographs published by Wordsong, Boyds Mills Press, Inc. Reprinted by permission. Excerpt from What is the World Made of?, by Kathleen Weidner Zoehfeld, illustrated by Paul Meisel. Text copyright © 1998 by Kathleen Weidner Zoehfeld. Illustrations copyright © 1998 by Paul Meisel. Reprinted by permission of HarperCollins Publishers. Excerpt from Big Freeze, by Catherine Chambers. Copyright © 2002 by Reed Educational & Professional Publishing. Reprinted by permission of Harcourt Education. Excerpt from Energy, Heat, Light, and Fuel, by Darlene Stille, illustrated by Sheree Boyd. Copyright © 2004 by Picture Window Books. Reprinted by permission of Picture Window Books.

Cover

(Seal pup) (Spine) Digital Vision/Getty Images. (Back cover seal) Daniel J. Cox/Getty Images. (Ice) Royalty-Free/CORBIS.

Photography

Unit A Opener: Bob Rozinski/Dancing Pelican. Florida Facts: (bkgd) Barbara Gerlach/Dembinsky Photo Associates, Inc. (tr) Dennis Macdonald/Photo Edit, Inc. (br) Joe McDonald/Corbis. (cr) Stan Osolinksi/Dembinsky Photo Associates, Inc. **A1** Len Kaufman Photography. **A4–A5** (bkgd) Yoshio Sawaraq/getty images. **A5** (t) Phil Degginger/Ed Degginger Photography. (bc) Christine M. Douglas/DK Images. **A6** (bl) Hans Reinhard/Bruce Coleman, Inc. **A6–A7** (bkgd) Birgit Koch/Alamy. **A8** Phil Degginger/Color Pic, Inc. **A9** (br) Rich Iwasaki/ Stone/Getty Images; (tr) Steve Gorton/DK Images. **A10** (bl) Matthew Ward/DK Images. (cl) Scott Camazine. (br) Heather Weston/ Botanica/ Getty Images. (c) Henry Beeker/Alamy. (tr) Peter Gardner/DK images. **A12** (bl) Rita Maas/Foodpix. **A12–A13** (bkgd) Michael P. Gadomski/Photo Researchers, Inc. **A16** (b David Young-Wolff/Photoedit, Inc. (cr) Clay Perry/Corbis. **A17** ©E.R. Degginger/Color-Pic, Inc. **A18–A19** (bkgd) Robert Holmgren/ Stone/Getty Images. **A19** (tr) Corbis; (tcl) Andy Crawford/DK Images. (tcr) Susanna Price/DK Images; (bcl) David Murray/DK Images. (bcr) Steve Gorton/DK Images. (bl) John Foxx/Alamy Images; (br) DK Images. (tl) Siede Preis/Photodisc/Getty Images. **A20** (bl) Matthew Ward/DK Images. **A20–A21** (bkgd) Balfour Studios/Alamy Images. **A24** (t) Darrell Gulin/DRK Photo. (c) John Gerlach/dembinsky Photo Associates. **A26** ©Phil Degginger/Ed Degginger Photography. **A28–A29** (bkgd) Johnny Johnson/AlaskaStock.com. **A29** (t) Masa Ushioda/Stephen Frink Collection/Alamy Images; (tc) Juniors Bildarchiv/ Alamy; (c) Suzanne L. & Joseph T. Collins/Photo Researchers, Inc. (b) ©R.R. Degginger/Color Pic, Inc. **A30** (tl) ©E.R. Degginger/Color Pic, Inc. (tr) S Solum/ Photo link/Photodisc/Getty Images. **A30–A31** (bkgd) Ingo Arndt/Foto Natura/Minden Pictures. **A32** Dave King/DK Images. **A33** (tc) Boch/Zefa/Masterfile; (tl) Nigel Dennis/Photo Researchers, Inc. (bc) ©E.R. Degginger/Color Pic, Inc.; (tr) Michael DeYoung/AlaskaStock.com. (bl) ©E.R. Degginger/Color Pic, Inc.; (tl) Tom Brakefield/Corbis. **A34–A35** (b) Masa ushioda/ Stephen Frink Collection/Alamy Images. **A35** (t) Joe Mcdonald/Corbis. (tl) Alan & Sandy Carey/ Photo Researchers, Inc. **A36** (b) Gail Shumway / Taxi/Corbis. **A37** Stephen Krasemann / Stone/Getty Images. **A38** (t) Laura Riley/ Bruce Coleman, Inc. **A38–A39** (bkgd) Greg Dimijian/ Photo Researchers, Inc. **A40** Juniors Bildarchiv/ Alamy. **A41** (tr) Larry Ditto/Bruce Coleman, Inc. (b) Larry Lipsky/DRK Photo. **A42** (tl) Suzanne L. & Joseph T. Collins/ Photo Researchers, Inc. (bl) Darren Maybury; Eye Ubiquitous/Corbis; br Georgette Douwma/ Photographer's Choice/Getty Images. **A43** (l) Jerry Young/D K Images. (r) Digital Vision/Getty Images. **A44–A45** Alan & Sandy Carey/Photo Researchers, Inc. **A46** ©E.R. Degginger/Color Pic, Inc. **A46–A47** (bkgd) George Herben/AlaskaStock.com **A47** (bl) ©E.R. Degginger/Color Pic, Inc.; (br) Suzanne L. Collins/Photo Researchers, Inc. **A48** Ardea. **A50** (l) Alan & Sandy Carey/Photo Researchers, Inc. (cl) Larry Ditto/Bruce Coleman, Inc. (c) Larry Lipsky/DRK Photo. (cr) ©E.R. Degginger/Color Pic, Inc. (r) Skip Moody/Dembinsky Photo Associates, Inc. **A52** (bkgd) David Zelick/Imagebank/Getty Images. **A53** (t) Larry Ditto/Bruce Coleman, Inc. (tc) Rommel/Masterfile. (bc) Pierre Arsenault/Masterfile. (b) Ted Wood/Imagebank/Getty Images. **A54–A55** (b) Olivier Ribardiere/Taxi/Getty Images. **A57** (tr) Phil Degginger/Color Pic, Inc. (tl) Chris King/DK Images. (cr) C Squared Studios/Photodisc/Getty Images. **A58** Ryan McVay/ Photodisc/Getty Images. **A59** (t) Steve Shott/DK Images. (l) Jose Luis Pelaez, Inc./Corbis. **A60** (tl) Jeff Greenberg/Photo Edit Inc. (br) Corbis. (tr) Rubberball Productions/Getty Images. **A61** (tl) Jeff Greenberg/Photoedit Inc. **A62** (bl) Simon Taplin/Asia Images Group. (frame) Image Farm Inc. **A62–63** (bkgd) Photo 24/Brand X Pictures/ Alamy. **A64** (br) Rommel/Masterfile. (bc) DK Images. **A65** (bl) Pierre Arsenault/Masterfile. (bc) Ryan Mcvay/ Photodisc/Getty Images. (br) Rubberball/Alamy Images. **A67** Richard hutchings/Photo Researchers, Inc. **A68** Myrleen Ferguson Cate/Photo Edit Inc. **A70** (r) Myrleen Ferguson Cate/Photo Edit Inc. (l) Carlos Davila/Superstock. **A72** Dominique Braud/Dembinsky Photo Associates, Inc. Unit B Opener: James D. Watt/Ocean Stock. Florida Facts: (bkgd) Al Petteway/National Geographic/Getty Images. (tr) Raymond Cramm/Photo Researchers, Inc. (cr) Florida Museum of Natural History. (br) Charles V. Angelo/Photo Researchers, Inc. **B1** Doug Perrine/Seapics. **B4–B5** Bermes/LAIF/Aurora. **B5** (bc) BananaStock/Picturequest. (b) Tom & Pat Leeson/Photo Researchers, Inc. (r) Eric Crichton / Bruce Coleman/Picturequest. (b) C Squared Studios / Photodisc/Getty Images. **B6** (tl) Brian Sytnyk/

Masterfile. (t) Photospin. **B6–B7** (bkgd) Arthur S. Aubry/Stone/Getty Images. **B8** (bc) Eric Crichton / Bruce Coleman/Picturequest. **B8–B9** (bkgd0 Ty Allison/Taxi/Getty Images. **B10** (br) Geri Engberg/The Image Works. (tc) Alan Pitcairn/Grant Heilman Photography. **B11** Norma Zuniga/Getty Images. **B14** (bl) Robert Lubeck/Animals Animals. **B14–B15** (bkgd) Kunst & Scheidulin/Premium/Panoramic Images. **B16** Liang Zhuoming/Corbis. **B17** (bc) J. H. Robinson/Photo Researchers, Inc. (br) Richard R. Hansen/Photo Researchers, Inc. (bl) Mark Gibson/Gibson Stock Photography. (tr) Arthur Morris/Corbis. (inset sun) SuperStock. **B18** (b) Steve Bloom/Taxi/Getty Images. (tr) Fotopic/Omni-Photo Communication. **B19** (b) Gerard Lacz/Animals Animals. (tr) Michael Boys/Corbis. **B20** (cr) Rick Sammon/Bruce Coleman Inc. (t) Tom & Pat Leeson/Photo Researchers, Inc. (b) Robert Brenner/Photo Edit, Inc. **B24–B25** (bkgd) Gregory G. Dimijian/Photo Researchers, Inc. **B25** (t) Peter Griffith/Masterfile. (tc) Garry Black/Mastefile. (bc) Ace Stock Limited/ Alamy. (b) F. Damm/Masterfile. **B26** (bl) S. Nielsen/DRK Photo. **B26–B27** (bkgd) J. David Andrews/Masterfile. **B29** Arco/P. Wegner/Alamy. **B30** (c) Tom & Pat Leeson/DRK Photo. (t) Joe McDonald/DRK Photo. (b) RO-MA Stock/Index Stock. **B31** (r) M. Fogden/Bruce Coleman. (b) Lynn M. Stone/ DRK Photo. **B32** Doug Perrine/DRK Photo. **B32–B33** (bkgd) M. Timothy O'Keefe/Bruce Coleman. **B36** Jerry Young/DK Images. **B38** (tr) Kevin Fleming/Corbis. **B38–39** (bkgd) Jim steinberg/Photo Researchers, Inc. **B39** (tr) Sovid Muench/Corbis. (bl) Mark Newman/Photo Researchers, Inc. **B40** (bl) ©E. R. Degginger/Color-Pic, Inc. **B40–B41** (bkgd) Bill Brooks/Masterfile. **B43** DK images. **B44** Linda Van Wijk/ MAsterfile. **B48** (l) Franklin Viola/Animals Animals. (c) Maresa Pryor/ Animals Animals. (r) G.I. Bernard/Photo Researchers, Inc. Unit C Opener: Tom Bean/DRK Photo. Florida Facts: (bkgd) Don Mason/Corbis. (tr) Maresa Pryor/Earth Scenes/Animals Animals. (cr) Juergen Christine Sohns/Earth Scenes/Animals Animals. (br) Raymond Patrick/Taxi/Getty Images. **C1** Tom Bean/DRK Photo. **C4–C5** (bkgd) Mark Newman/Bruce Coleman. **C5** (t) ©Dwight Kuhn/Dwight Kuhn Photography. (b) Gary Retherford/Photo Researchers, Inc. (tc) Harry Taylor/DK images. **C6** (bl) D. Hurst/Alamy. **C6–C7** (bkgd) Mark Windom/Index Stock. **C10** (tl) ©E.R. Degginger/Color Pic, Inc. (tr) ©E.R. Degginger/Color Pic, Inc. (cr) Dave King/DK Images. (tr) Wolfgang Kaehler/Corbis. **C11** Paul Barton/Corbis. **C12** (bl) ©E. R. Degginger/Bruce Coleman, Inc. **C12–C13** (bkgd) S. Solum/Photolink/Getty Images. **C14** (r) DK Images. **C14** (c) ©E.R. Degginger/Color Pic, Inc. (l) Cherles D. Winters/Photo Reasearchers. **C15** (tcr) DK Images. (l) Andreas Einsiedel/DK images. (b) © E. R Degginger/Dembinsky Photo Associates. (tr) Stephen J Krasemann/Drk photo. (cr) Harry Taylor/DK Images. **C16** (br) Ben Johnson/ Science Photo Library/Getty Images. (tcr) Harry Taylor/DK images. (tr) Colin Keates/DK images. (tcl) Superstock. (bcl) Charles d. Winters/Photo Researchers, Inc. (bl) Jack Sullivanq/Alamy Images. **C17** (r) Adrian Muttitt/Alamy Images. (l) Stephen J Krasemann/DRK Photo. **C22** (bl) S.L. Francisco Ontanon/The Image Bank/Getty Images. **C22–C23** (bkgd) Andreas Stirnberg/The Image Bank/Getty Images. **C25** (l) © Dwight Kuhn/Bruce Coleman, Inc. (r) Holt Studios/Nigel Catlin/Photo Researchers, Inc. **C26** (r) Wayne Lawler/Photo Researchers, Inc. (l) James Randklev/ChromoSohm Media Inc./Photo Researchers, Inc. **C28** (bl) Gary Black/Masterfile. (tr) ©E. R. Degginger Color Pic, Inc. (tl) Mark Windom/Index stock. **C30–C31** (bkgd) Richard Levine/Alamy Images. **C31** (r) Michelle D. Bridwell/Photo Edit, Inc. (tc) Ken Graham/Bruce Coleman Inc. (b) Eric Fowke/Photo Edit, Inc. **C32–C33** (bkgd) Photri. **C34** Comstock Images/Getty Images **C35** (tr) Jack W. Dykinga/Bruce Coleman, Inc. (b) Lawrence migdale/Photo Researchers, Inc. **C36** (t) Michelle D. Bridwell/Photo Edit, Inc. (b) Jeff Greenberg/Photo Edit, Inc. **C37** Steve Heller/AP Wide World Photo. **C38** (bl) Cathy Melloan Resources/Photo Edit, Inc. **C38–C39** (bkgd) C. C. Lockwood/DRK Photo. **C40** (bl) Myrleen Ferguson Cate/Photo Edit, Inc. (r) SW productions/ Getty images. **C41** (b) Doug Martin/Photo Researchers, Inc. (tr) David Schmidt/Masterfile. (br) Wernher Krutein/Photovault. **C42** (t) Ken Graham/Bruce Coleman, Inc. (cl) Johnathan Nourok/Photo Edit Inc. **C43** © Jonathan Nourok/Photo Edit. **C44–C45** (bkgd) Mark Gibson. **C46** (t) Comstock Images. **C46–C47** (bkgd) Michael Wickes/Bruce Coleman, Inc. **C48** (bc) Patrick Palunbo/Wildlife Creations International USA. **C49** (t) Michael Newman/Photo Edit, Inc. **C50** (bl) Eric Fowke/Photo Edit, Inc. (br) ©E.R. Degginger/Color Pic, Inc. **C51** (tr) Michael newman/Photo Edit, Inc. (cr) Michael D. L. Jordan/Dembinsky Photo Associates, Inc. (cl) Dennis MacDonald/Photo Edit, Inc. (b) © Photo Courtesy of Nike, Inc. **C54** (cr) Eric Fowke/Photo Edit, Inc. (l) C. C. Lockwood/DRK Photo. **C56** (l) Mark A. Scneider/Dembinsky Photo Associates, Inc. (c) Mark A. Scneider/Dembinsky Photo Associates, Inc. (r) © E.R. Degginger/ Dembinsky Photo Associates, Inc. Unit D Opener: Adam Jones Photography. Florida Facts: (bkgd) Rick Runion/The Ledger/Corbis. (tr) Charles Moran/Silver Image. (br) Richard Llune/Corbis. (cr) Reuters/ Corbis. **D1** (b) S. Nielsen/DRK Photo. **D4–D5** (bkgd) Alan Schein Photography/Corbis. **D5** (t) Ariel SKelley/Corbis. (bc) Tom BEan/DRK Photo. (bl) © E. R. Degginger/Color Pic, Inc. (tl) David Carriere/Index Stock Images. (br) Leonard Lee Ruell/Earth Scenes. (tr) George E. Jones 111/Photo Researchers, Inc. **D6** (bl) Ariel Skelley/Corbis. **D6–D7** (bkgd) Stephen St. John/ National Geographic/Getty Images. **D8** Michael Newman/Photo Edit, Inc. **D9** (r) Ariel Skelley/Corbis. (l) Douglas Peebles/ Corbis. **D10** © Copyright 2001 Cynthia Malaran http://www.malaran. com from the website http://www.watchingthechanges.com All Rights Reserved. **D11** Robert Glusic/Photodisc/Getty Images. **D12** (bl) Robert Holmes/Corbis. **D12–D13** (bkgd) Burgess Blevins/Getty Images. **D14** Jeff Cadge/ The Image Bank/Getty Images. **D15** AJA Productions/The Image Bank/Getty Images. **D16** (br) Jeff Greenberg/Photo Edit, Inc. (bl) David Young-Wolff/Photo Edit, Inc. **D17** (r) David Young-Wolff/Photo Edit, Inc. (cr) Tony Freeman/Photo Edit, Inc. **D20–D21** (bkgd) Craig Tuttle/Corbis **D22–D23** (bkgd) Jim Steinberg/Photo Researchers, Inc. **D24** (c) Royalty-free/Corbis. **D24–D25** (bkgd) Terry Eggers/Panoramic Images. **D25** (tl) Tom Bean/DRK Photo. (r) Brock May/Photo Researchers Inc. **D26** (bl) Kim Taylor and Jane burton/DK images **D26–D27** (bkgd) Peter Adams Photography/Alamy Images **D28** Peter Dean/ Stone/Getty Images **D29** (b) © Dwight Kuhn. (bc) Bob Jensen/Bruce Coleman Inc. (br) Dynamic Graphics Group/Creatas/Alamy Images. (tr) Julie Habel/Corbis. **D30** (b) Ariel Skelley/Corbis. (tl) Ed Young/Corbis. **D31** Premium Stock/Corbis. **D32** (bl) Siede Preis/ Photodisc/Getty Images. **D32–D33** (bkgd) Julio Lopez Saguar/Photonica. **D34** Ron Chapple/Thinkstock/Getty Images. **D35** (br) © Dwight Kuhn. (r) William h. Mullins/Photo Researchers, Inc. **D36** (b) Steve Skjold/Photo Edit, Inc. **D37** Thomas Mangelsen/Minden Pictures **D38** (b) © E.R. Degginger/ Color Pic, Inc. (r) Leonard Lee Ruell/Earth Scenes. (t) George E. Jones 111/Photo Researchers, Inc. (l) David Carriere/Index Stock Imagery. **D42–D43** (bkgd) Paul & Linda Marie Ambrose/Getty Images. **D43** (t) Gerard Lacz/Animals Animals. (tc) Nora Good/MAsterfile. (bc) Corbis. **D44** (b) Raymond Tercafs/Bruce Coleman Inc. **D44–D45** (t) Don Farrall/ Photodisc/Getty images. (b) Terry Thompson/Panoramic Images. (c) Dallos and John Heaton/Alamy Images. **D46** D. Robert & Lorri Franz/Corbis. **D47** (b) E. R. Degginger/Bruce Coleman Inc. (tr) GERARD LACZ/Animals Animals. **D48–D49** B.a.e. Inc./Alamy Images. **D50** (bl) Rettinghaus/Zefa/Masterfile. **D50–D51** (bkgd) Bill Brooks/ Masterfile. **D56** (bl) S. neilsen/DRK Photo. **D56–D57** (bkgd) Chris Cook/ Photo Researchers, Inc. **D58–D59** NASA/Bruce Coleman inc. **D60** (r) S. Neilsen/DRK photo. **D60–D61** (bkgd) Taxi/Getty Images. **D61** (l) S. Neilsen/DRK photo. (r) S. Neilsen/DRK photo. **D62** (tl) Time Life Pictures/ Getty Images. (br) Corbis. **D63** (t) Kennedy Space Center/NASA. (bl) NASA. **D64** (bl) Marc Epstein/DRK Photo. **D64–D65** (bkgd) Michael Thompson/Animals Animals. **D65** (t) bkgd) Martien Mulder/Stone/Getty Images. (b bkgd) Martien Mulder/Stone/Getty Images. **D66** (bl) Myrleen Ferguson Photo Edit, Inc. (br) Eric Fowke/Photo Edit, Inc. **D67** (bl) Ariel Skelley/Corbis. (bc) Jeff Zaruba / Corbis. (br) DiMaggio/ Kalish/Corbis. **D72** (l) David Stoecklein/Corbis. **D72** (c) Randy Faris/ Corbis. **D72** (r) Larry Gilpin/ Stone/Getty Images. Florida Facts: (bkgd) Tony Arruza/Corbis. (cr) Michael Schwartz/The Image Works. (tr) Don Smetzer/Photo Edit, Inc. (br) Kevin Fleming/Corbis. **E1** Michele Stapleton/Michele Stapleton Photography. **E4–E5** (bkgd) Roy Morsch/ Corbis. **E5** (tc) Robert George Young/Masterfile. (bc) C. Sagel/ Masterfile. (t) Image Source/Alamy Images. **E8** Jade Lee/ Asia Images/ Getty Images. **E6–E7** (bkgd) Peter Christopher/Masterfile. **E9** (c) Dave King/Dk Images. (r) Steve Shott/DK Images. **E10** (tr) Image Source/ Alamy Images. (b) Brand X Pictures/Getty Images. **E11** (bl) Corbis. (tl) Spencer Jones/ Foodpix/getty Images. (tr) Dave King/D.K. Images. (br) Dk Images. **E12–E13** (bkgd) Valerie Simmons/Masterfile. **E17** Martin Hanke/ Bildagentur Franz Waldhaeusl/Alamy Images. **E26** (bl) Dynamic

Graphics/Picturequest. **E30** (br) Sie de Preis/ Photodisc/Getty images. (bl) Siedie Preis/ Photodisc/Getty Images. **E34–E35** (bkgd) Kwame Zikomo/Age FotoStock America Inc. **E35** (t) GK & Vikki Hart/Getty Images. (b) Christina Kennedy/photo edit inc. (tc) Steve Cole/Getty images. (tr) Dynamic Graphics/Creatas. **E36–E37** (bkgd) JC Carton/ Bruce Colman Inc. **E42** (bl) Stephen Shepard/Alamy Images. **E42–E43** (bkgd) Pekka, Parviainen/Photo Researchers, Inc. **E44** Michael Newman/ Photo Edit, Inc. **E45** (t) Stephen G. Maka/DRK Photo. (c) Stephen G. Maka/DRK Photo. (b) Stephen G. Maka/DRK photo. (t) Chee Meng Ng/ Chee Meng Ng Photography. **E46** (c) Chee Meng Ng/Chee Meng Ng Photography. (br) Daniel Barillot/Masterfile. **E47** Wayne Eastep/Stone/ Getty Images. **E53** (br) Adam Woolfitt/Alamy. Unit F Opener: Jeff Greenberg/The Image Works. Florida Facts: (bkgd) Gail Mooney/ Masterfile. (cr) Milton Fullman. (tr) Cleo Photography/Photo Edit, Inc. (br)Tom Wagner/Courtesy of Busch Gardens Tampa Bay. **F1** Baby Face/ PictureQuest. **F4–F5** (bkgd) Jeff Hunter/The Image Bank/Getty Images. **F5** (t) Daniel Barillot/Masterfile. (tc) Harald Sund/The Image Bank/Getty Images. (b) Michael Newman/Photo Edit, Inc. **F6–F7** (bkgd) Goodshot/ Alamy Images. **F8** Richard T. Nowitz/Corbis. **F9** (t) Alchemy/Alamy images. (lc) Lennox Hearth Products. **F10** (tl) Reuters/Corbis. (b) Daniel Barillot/Masterfile. **F12** (bl) Stuart Westmorland/Stone/Getty Images. **F12–F13** (bkgd) Mark Gibson. **F14** Harald Sund/The Image Bank/ Getty Images. **F15** (tr) ©E.R. Degginger/Color Pic, Inc. (br ©Phil Degginger/Color Pic, Inc. **F17** (tr) C Squared Studio/Photodisc/Getty Images. **F18** (b) Michael & Patricia Fogden/Minden pictures. **F18–F19** (bkgd) Gunter Ziesler/Peter Arnold, Inc. **F20** Nasa. **F21** (t) Gregory Scott/DK Images. **F23** Michael Newman/Photo Edit, Inc. **F24–F25** Michael Newman/Photo Edit, Inc. **F26** Steve Shott/DK Images. **F27** (tr) David Young-Wolff/Photo Edit Inc. (b) Michael Newman/Photo Edit, Inc. **F28** (tl) Sciencephotos/Alamy images. (c) Philip Rostron/Masterfile. **F29** CORBIS. (tbr) Getty Images. **F30** (l) Harald Sund/ The Image Bank/ Getty Images. **F30** (c) Alchemy/Alamy Images. **F32–F33** (bkgd) JOn Eisberg / Taxi/Getty Images. **F33** (br) Myrleen ferguson Cate/Photo Edit, Inc. **F34–F35** Blair Seitz/Photo Researchers Inc. **F38** (bl) ©E.R. Degginger/Color Pic Inc. (c) ©E.R. Degginger//Color Pic Inc. **F39** (cr) Photofusion Picture Library/Alamy Images. (tl) Jeff Greenberg/Photo Edit Inc. (tc) ©E.R. Degginger/Color Pic Inc. **F40** (bl) Myrleen Ferguson Cate/Photo Edit, Inc. **F40–41** (bkgd) Joseph Sohm/ChomoSohm Inc./ Corbis. **F42** (bl) Foodcollection/Alamy images. (br) Tom Szuba/ Masterfile. **F44** Alan & Linda Detrick/Photo Researchers Inc. **F46** (cr) Ken Cavanagh/Photo Researchers Inc. **F46** (cr) Judith Jango-Cohen. **F47** (c) Andrew Itkoff/Silver Image. **F48–F49** Greg Stott/Masterfile. **F54** (c) Foodcollection/Alamy images. (rc) Tom Szuba/ Masterfile. **F56** Reuters/Corbis.

Assignment

A6, A7, A12, A13, ©Hmco/Richard Hutchings Photography. **A21, A30, A31, A38, A39, A44. A45,** ©Hmco/Ken Karp Photography. **A54, A55, A56, A57** ©Hmco/Richard Hutchings Photography. **A62, A63, A66,** ©Hmco/Ken Karp Photography. **A70** ©Hmco/Richard Hutchings Photography. **B6, B7** ©Hmco/Richard Hutchings Photography. **C12, C13** ©Hmco/Ken Karp Photography. **B14, B15, B26** ©Hmco/Richard Hutchings Photography. **B27** ©Hmco/Lawrence Migdale. **B32, B33** ©Hmco/Ken Karp Photography. **B40, B41,** ©Hmco/Richard Hutchings Photography. **C5** ©Hmco/Ken Karp Photography. **C6, C7, C12** ©Hmco/Richard Hutchings Photography. **C18, C20** ©Hmco/Ken Karp Photography. **C22, C23** ©Hmco/Richard Hutchings Photography. **C24, C28, C31** ©Hmco/Ken Karp Photography. **C32, C33, C38, C39, C46, C47** ©Hmco/Richard Hutchings Photography. **C48, C50** ©Hmco/Ken Karp Photography. **C52** ©Hmco/Richard Hutchings Photography. **C45** (r) ©Hmco/Richard Hutchings Photography. (lc) ©Hmco/Ken Karp Photography. **D7, D13, D20, D21,** ©Hmco/Ken Karp Photography. **D26, D27,** ©Hmco/Richard Hutchings Photography. **D32, D33, D43** ©Hmco/ Ken Karp Photography. **D44** ©Hmco/Richard Hutchings Photography. **D45, D49** ©Hmco/Ken Karp Photography. **D50** ©Hmco/Richard Hutchings Photography. (b) ©Hmco/Ken Karp Photography. **D51** ©Hmco/ Ken Karp Photography. **D56** (cr) ©Hmco/Ken Karp Photography, (c) ©Hmco/Richard Hutchings Photography. **D57, D63, D65** ©Hmco/Richard Hutchings Photography. **E5** ©Hmco/Ken Karp Photography. **E6, E7,** ©HMCo/Richard Hutchings Photography. **E12** ©HMCo/Richard Hutchings Photography. (b) ©HMCo/Ken Karp Photography. **E13** ©HMCo/Richard Hutchings Photography. **E14, E15, E16** ©HMCo/Ken Karp Photography. **E18, E19, E20, E21** ©HMCo/Richard Hutchings Photography. **E24, E25** ©HMCo/Ken Karp Photography. **E26, E27** ©HMCo/Richard Hutchings Photography. **E28, E29** ©HMCo/Ken Karp Photography. **E36, E37,** ©HMCo/Richard Hutchings Photography. **E40** ©HMCo/Ken Karp Photography. **E42, E43,** ©HMCo/Richard Hutchings Photography. **E48** ©HMCo/Richard Hutchings Photography, (bl) ©Hmco/Bud Endress Photography. **E48–E49** (bkgd) ©Hmco/Bud Endress Photography. **E50, E51** ©Hmco/Bud Endress Photography. **E52** ©HMCo/Ken Karp Photography. **F3** ©Hmco/ Ken Karp Photography. **F6, F7** ©Hmco/Richard Hutchings Photography. **F9** ©Hmco/Lawrence Migdale. **F11** ©Hmco/Ken Karp Photography. **F12, F13** ©Hmco/Richard Hutchings Photography. **F15** ©Hmco/Ken Karp Photography. **F16** ©Hmco/Lawrence Migdale. **F18, F19** ©Hmco/Richard Hutchings Photography. **F21** ©Hmco/Lawrence Migdale. **F22** ©Hmco/ Ken Karp Photography. **F24, F25, F29** ©Hmco/Richard Hutchings Photography. **F30** ©Hmco/Ken Karp Photography. **F33** ©Hmco/Lawrence Migdale. **F34, F35, F40, F41, F46, F47, F48, F49** ©Hmco/Richard Hutchings Photography. **F52** ©HMCo/Lawrence Migdale.

Illustration

A5, A22, A23 Pat Rossi Calkin. **B12–B13** John Berg. **B22** Terri Chicko. **B28–B29, B34–B3, B36–B37, B42–B43** Richard Cowdrey. **B46** Terri Chicko. **C8–C9** Phil Wilson. **C18–C19, C20–21** Cheryl Mendenhall. **C25** Phil Wilson. **C53** Robert Schuster. **D5, D16, D17** Promotion Studios. **D29** Steve McEntee. **D52–53, D54–D55, D59, D66–D67, Bell Melvin. D68** Patrick Gnan. **D69** Laura Ovresat. **D70** Bill Melvin. **E17** Promotion Studios. **E32, E54** Terri Chicko. **E56** Patrick Gnan. **F43** Mircea Catusanu. **F46–F47** Steve Costanza.

Nature of Science

PHOTOGRAPHY: (kangaroo) © Martin Rugner/age Fototock. **S1** © Digital Vision. **S2-3** © Tim Sloan/AFP/Getty. **S3** (r) Photo courtesy of the National Museum of the American Indian, Smithsonian Institution. **S4-5** © HMCo./Joel Benjamin Photography. **S6-7** © HMCo./Ed Imaging. **S8-9** © HMCo./Ed Imaging. **S10** Julie Dermody. **S11** © Issei Kato/ Reuters/Corbis. **S12** © HMCo./Joel Benjamin Photography. **S14** © HMCo./Joel Benjamin Photography. **S16** © HMCo./Richard Hutchings Photography.

Health and Fitness Handbook

ASSIGNMENT: **H12, H13,** © HMCo./Coppola Studios Inc. **H15, H17** © HMCo./Joel Benjamin. ILLUSTRATION: **H12, H13,** Bart Vallecoccia. **H17** Linda Lee.

Science and Math Toolbox

H7 (t) John Giustina/Getty Images. (m) Georgette Douwma/Getty Images. (b) Giel/Getty Images. **H8** Photodisc/Getty Images.